THE PAPER TIDE

and other stories

by

Tom Fewer

Ballylough Books

THE PAPER TIDE

First Published in 2005

Copyright © Tom Fewer, 2005

ISBN 0-9533704-6-1

The Great Man, *The Vigil*, and *Paddy* were originally published
by *The Munster Express.*

Published by Ballylough Books
Callaghane, Co. Waterford, Ireland
'phone: 00353 51 382538
e-mail: ballyloughbooks@eircom.net
web site : www.ardkeen.ie/ballyloughbooks

Printed by
Modern Printers Ltd
Loughboy Industrial Estate, Kilkenny.
056-7721739

Ballylough Books

THE PAPER TIDE

Tom Fewer was born in Waterford, Ireland where he now
lives, having worked in the UK, Canada and Bermuda
for eleven years. He is the author of *Waterford People:*

By the same Author

WATERFORD PEOPLE – *A Biographical Dictionary*
ISBN 0-9533704-4-5

I WAS A DAY IN WATERFORD – *An Anthology of Writing about Waterford City and County from the 18th to the 20th Century (Editor and compiler).*
ISBN – 9533704-1-0

2

For my good friend *C.A.H.*

Contents	Page

NUMBER NINE

During the late 1940s, when Tim Doyle was just a toddler, his family lived in one of a terrace of nondescript, early Victorian houses crammed into a narrow, dusty, and busy street just outside the commercial district of the town. The houses were dull and without frills of any kind. The Doyle's house, which was Number Nine, was a solid but dark, four-storied building made all the more gloomy by the fact that it, and all the other houses in the narrow street, existed in an almost permanent cloud of coal dust, courtesy of the busy coal merchant who carried on his trade there. The street also boasted a substantial bakery, so that anyone leaving by the front door immediately had the scent of fresh, crusty bread and the taste of dusty coal.

The front door of Number Nine was ancient and massive and totally beyond the powers of any mere child. Sometimes, when Tim heard the bang of the big knocker, he would run to the dark hall, sliding on the polished linoleum, in time to see Katie pull back the old fashioned bolt and ease the door open, squinting her eyes to avoid the swirl of dust, and allowing a cacophony of street sounds to enter the house.

It was especially noisy when the steam whistle had blown at the timber mill in the next street, and the workers surged home on foot and cycle, joined by their colleagues from the bakery, and schoolboys from the rival Christian Brothers and De La Salle Brothers schools nearby.

The living-room and dining room led off from the hall and for natural light relied on the sunlight reflected from the building opposite. The remainder of the ground floor had all the usual offices of a nineteenth century house—kitchen, pantry, scullery and larder; and, opening on to the backyard, the coal house. The yard also contained a little construction with fine mesh windows on a pole that looked like a dovecote but was in fact a meat-safe, and, in the absence of refrigerators in the nineteen-forties, was used for short term storage of cooked meat.

The first floor, where the family slept, contained three bedrooms and the bathroom.

The second floor also contained three bedrooms, one of which was occupied by Katie, who had come in from the country as a live-in maid at the age of fifteen.

The top floor was totally unfurnished and unoccupied apart from spiders and ghosts. For children it was very scary, and no child would venture up there alone.

It was a draughty house, full of creaking floorboards and unexplained cracks and gaps in the plasterwork, from which mice and other rodents made regular forays.

One night, not long after they had moved in, when Tim was still a baby and slept in a cot, his mother, hearing him crying, came into his room to find his face covered in blood, and a rat scurrying under the skirting board. Her screams brought his father running. After a quick glance at the situation, his father ran downstairs, jumped on his bicycle and cycled furiously across town for the doctor. After much high drama, it was eventually discovered that the rat had gnawed at the child's finger as his hand dangled from the cot. He had then rubbed his bloody little hand all over his face.

In later life Tim had no recollection of this happening but still carried the small white, curved scars of teethmarks on the middle finger of his right hand.

But there was another traumatic experience, the memory of which would come back to him many years later.

In the February of his fourth year, the days were so short that the house seemed to be full of dark corners.

On one of these days, all the adults in the house appeared to be very busy and had no time for him.

"Shush now," he was told, "go play with your toys."

There was a small room between the dining room and the kitchen where he kept his toys, and here he hunkered disconsolately, running a Dinky Toy car along the ubiquitous linoleum in the light of a weak electric bulb. From time to time, Katie would look in to see if he was behaving himself. The linoleum was cold and the winter wind made itself felt in fierce scudding draughts under the door.

After a while he became bored with his toys and toddled out to the warm kitchen to seek company. The shiny black stove glowed but there was no one in the room. He wandered through the dining room into the front hall and looked up the stairs. The house was silent. A weak, grey light came through the rounded window on the landing and was reflected in the brass carpet rods on the stairs. Katie was nowhere to be seen.

Slowly he edged himself up the stairs, hanging on to the banisters for support. After two flights, he was facing the door of his mother's bedroom. At least he always thought of it as his mother's bedroom, although it was equally his father's of course. But Dad, though kindly, seemed a somewhat brusque and authoritarian figure with harsh, bristly cheeks, who smelled of toothpaste and Silvikrin Hair Oil, and who made brief, god-like appearances at different times in the day.

His mother on the other hand, was the soft and sweet-smelling fountain of all good things, patient to an almost infinite degree, and a great understander of the strange mysteries that worry a four-year-old.

The door was large and heavy and made of pine. The round, hardwood knob was almost too difficult for his chubby hands to turn, but after standing on tiptoe and gasping a great deal it finally did.

The door swung slowly open and revealed a scene which he would not immediately understand and which he would only remember many years later.

The end of his mother's carved mahogany bed was in front of him. The head of the bed was against the far wall and on each side of it a window looked out on the back garden. On the windows, dark red, velvet curtains were partly drawn, and the weak February sun filtered into the room. His mother lay on the bed, her legs apart and her two knees jutting up. Leaning over her was Doctor O'Keefe, his shirtsleeves rolled up, some instrument glinting in his hand, the sun reflecting on his smooth oiled hair and round spectacles as he turned and looked at Tim.

"Out, boy, out!" he half whispered, half shouted at

him.

For an instant, Tim just stood there, not understanding what was happening, the scene somehow recalling a kitchen maid's fairy story. Then he turned and ran, by some miracle reaching the end of the stairs without mishap.

Later Katie found him, hunched over his toy-box, seemingly engrossed in his lead soldiers and tanks.

Many years later the scene would come back to him, and he would understand that he had been an unwitting witness to the birth of his brother, Michael.

Decades later, when his parents had both died and he was the owner of the house, he converted it into flats. The door to his mother's bedroom was removed during the conversion, and for some reason he took it home, meaning to use it again at some stage.

One failed marriage and two homes later, he still had the door. It served briefly as a temporary stable door and on another occasion protected a litter of pups in the corner of a barn, but most of the time it just gathered dust in several sheds and garages.

Finally, Tim had it stripped down to the original old pine. He oiled and polished it, and converted it into a headboard for his bed.

Now, just occasionally, in the late hours of a restless night, when sleep is slow to come, his hand brushes the smooth wood, and he thinks of that day, so long ago, and of his mother.

PADDY

It was a typical Irish farmhouse of the nineteen-thirties. Built of solid concrete blocks, with a slate roof, it sat on a hill overlooking the farm. From the road it looked private, quaint, homely and comfortable; protected and cosseted by trees and shrubs. Nothing exotic, just common trees available to the penny-poor farmer of the times; sycamore, ash, laurel, flowering raspberry and some shrubs whose identities had died with his grandparents.

The house was surrounded by modest, but well-built farm buildings constructed from rough red sandstone. They had been well cared for down through the years, their slates now secured by a coating of tar, their doors a mixture of wood, dark paint and various coats of preservative. The well-greased bolts on the outhouse doors were set at an angle so that there was no danger of them sliding open by accident.

A huge pile of green ash and dead elm boughs occupied one corner of the yard near the chopping block. Nearby, a rusty but sturdy lean-to barn contained a collection of relatively modern as well as ancient and obsolete farm machinery, all kept against the day they might come in handy, along with a small, gray Massey-Ferguson tractor in perfect condition.

In its day, during the wartime, and for years afterwards, the house had been the pride of the neighbourhood. Its solid concrete walls and tall ceilings contrasted with the earthen walls of older houses, yet it retained many of the old features of the traditional Irish farmhouse, including the great open fireplace in which a tall man could stand upright and look at the sky. A Pierce blower was in regular use. In later years, a Rayburn solid fuel cooker had been installed opposite the fireplace, and on very cold winter nights both were sometimes kept blazing.

The family of six gradually dwindled. Two daughters and a son married and moved away, leaving the youngest child, Paddy, with the elderly parents.

Paddy was generally regarded as wild. Small and wiry in stature, with dark red hair and a perpetual grin, he was mischievous and inquisitive, but had the wisdom and know-how that often seems to be the gift of the youngest child.

Every day he arose early with his father. Together they gathered in the cows and milked them. In those days tractors were still rare enough, and the creamery had yet to acquire a tanker. When the milking was finished, Bill, a wise little draft horse, would be put between the shafts of a two-wheeled cart, onto which Paddy and his father would manhandle the churns of fresh milk. They would then mount the front of the cart, his father would flick the reins, and Bill would trot off down to the creamery.

When the weather was good Paddy loved that trip. With a folded jute sack under his bottom to soften the vibrations (his father was slow to change to rubber wheels) and the horse hacking on at a good clip, he felt on top of the world.

On arrival at the creamery they off-loaded the churns onto the concrete platform. While the milk was being tested and the churns emptied and washed, Bill would be moored to one of the rings in the wall while Paddy and his father went to the Co-op shop to buy the necessary basics of life; bread, tea, sugar and whatever else was on his mother's shopping list. Paddy would invariably persuade his father to part with a penny with which he would buy himself a liquorice blackjack or a couple of half-penny squares of the hardest toffee Cleeves ever made. If the weather was fine he would sit on the wall, sucking and chewing his gob-stopper and listening to the talk of his father and the other farmers, and soaking in the lore of the land.

He loved the summers and the harvests and as he grew stronger he would be in the thick of it, forking hay and straw from morning 'til evening, doing the work of a man twice his size. As a child he had loved the threshing, and when not much more than a toddler, was stationed with other small children in the grain loft over the milking parlour. Each time the threshing machine filled a bag of oats, the bag was carried on the shoulder of one of the young men, up the ladder to the loft. Then the youngsters' job was to grab the sack, and, with great squealing and shouting, pull it along the floor— wonderfully smooth and shiny from years of use—to the back of the loft and empty it onto a growing mountain.

By the time he was fifteen, the toffee had given way to the surreptitious Woodbine, and once he had reached his late teens no dance, wake or wedding would be complete without his presence.

The social life of the area centered, of course, on the local public house, a solid, deep-walled, thatched building standing squarely at the crossroads. It was a marvellously cosy place, its thick walls and dense thatch blocking out the problems of the world outside, the storms and gales, and, with increasing frequency, the crashes of cars and sometimes lorries on the sharp bend, which, on more than one occasion threatened to wipe out the pub and all within.

The ancestry of the pub went back to the early nineteenth century, though in truth very little had changed over the years. The public bar was a room situated in the middle of the house. On one side of it was the family sitting room and on the other the kitchen. The crudely carved but handsome wood paneling which surrounded the bar had become smooth and noble over the years, its simple decoration (made, it was said, with a clasp-knife) caressed by time and numerous coats of varnish.

The large fireplace had devoured forests in its time and still welcomed great logs into its lap. The ancient counter, a single massive beam of pitch pine said to have come from a shipwreck, gleamed from infinite applications of alcohol and horny hands, its grain pushing upward from the darker pith. At one end of it, a small private area, for the totting up of customers orders, was shielded by a glass partition, made more private by the addition to the glass of star-patterned wax paper. Also at this end, for as far back as anyone could remember, stood a Grundig radio, for at least a generation the pride of the proprietor. Many an All-Ireland had been listened to on it, by hard-working country men taking a break from the harvest, their sunburned faces agleam with expectation, their work-worn hands clasping large bottles of Guinness or small glasses of whiskey.

Between the door and the partition was a short bench or form, and here in due course Paddy took what was to become his usual place. His occupancy of it would become as regular as that of a long-serving member of the Dáil.

On taking his seat "the usual" would be ordered. Then greetings and blessings would be exchanged, the weather reviewed, its future behavior predicted, and the progress of various crops and harvests commented on.

Politics would also be touched on, but not in depth, the general consensus being that it was better not to say too much; you never knew when you might need some help in getting a grant, and in any case, the present lot were as bad as the last lot.

As the evening went on, and more pints were consumed, the conversation became more lively.

In the course of time Paddy's parents passed away and he became the sole occupant of the home place, as he like to call it. He worked hard tilling land and milking cows. From time to time he would add some improvement to the farm, planting a grove of conifer trees to fend off the north winds, or concreting the paths to and from the farmyard. When work was finished at the end of the week, he washed and dressed himself up and took off for any dance that might be on in the neighbourhood, and indeed there were many dances in those times, at crossroads and village halls.

An occasion he loved was the annual threshing in his own haggard. All the neighbours came, and while the men raised dust and sweat outside, the women set up trestle tables in the big kitchen and prepared a hearty dinner. At midday, Paddy would call a halt to the work and the men would wash their hands in the big barrel under the gutter, and shuffle eagerly into the house.

In the comparative gloom of the cool kitchen, clouds

of steam arose from small mountains of unpeeled cooked potatoes piled in the centre of each table, as large plates of meat and vegetables were passed around to the men. Pots of tea followed but Paddy made sure that there was always a crate or two of Guinness to wash the food down. On these occasions, the *craic* was mighty, and Paddy, with a glass in one hand, and a fag in the other, was the life and soul of the party.

Apart from being popular, Paddy was an eligible bachelor and for his part liked nothing better than chatting up the girls. But beneath it all he was a shy man, and although his manoeuvres were magnificent, he never really engaged the enemy, except for one or two slight skirmishes outside the dance hall. Instead, he invariably left the company with a witty remark and a grin, whipped on his trouser clips, mounted his Raleigh bicycle and quickly disappeared into the night.

And then, one day, he met Betty Keogh.

Betty was nursing in the hospital in the nearby town, but she had cousins in Paddy's part of the countryside and used to visit them regularly on her Lambretta scooter. The two met at one of the local dances and immediately got on like a house on fire. She actually got him to venture onto the dance floor where everyone was surprised to discover that he was quite a good dancer. She had a sense of humour which fully appreciated his droll stories and jokes. Paddy had never had such a beautiful listener.

Soon the two would arrange to meet each other at all the local festive occasions. She would arrive on her scooter and he would be close behind her on his Raleigh (there was no way he would take a lift on the scooter). He quickly realised that there was no future in this arrangement and turned up at the pub one summer's evening with a second-hand Ford car. Everyone came out of the pub to look at it, to try the seats and the steering wheel, and gently kick the tyres. They all wished him well wear of it and returned to the bar to reflect in some wonder at the turn of events.

Soon Paddy and Betty were seen everywhere; at the pictures, walking on the strand at the seaside, and even at the races in Clonmel.

There were rumours of an engagement, but the true facts of it could not be got out of Paddy by means of any subterfuge, and he firmly discouraged any direct questions on the subject. But something was going on, his friends agreed. And, although Paddy dropped in to the pub on a regular, even daily basis, he seemed to be drinking less and had cut down on the fags, too. He was always in great form, and took pride in his Ford car, which he kept spotless.

Then came a time when neither Betty nor Paddy were to be seen anywhere. Paddy's seat in the pub was unoccupied from one week to the next. People smiled or winked and remarked coyly how lovers tended to become so absorbed in themselves that they forgot all about their friends.

That summer was one of the glorious ones that Ireland seems to get in one year out of ten. Inevitably there was a drought, and at Sunday Mass prayers were offered for rain, while in Dublin the corridors of power became silent except for the buzz of trapped bluebottles, as the deputies enjoyed the Galway Races and the Dublin Horse Show, where huge crowds watched the show-jumping while the bars rang to the sound of laughter and the clink of glasses.

The beaches were thronged, and ice-cream sales soared with the temperature.

All across the country hurlers and footballers turned out on sun-hardened pitches as each team fought for a place in the final at Croke Park.

July and half of August went by, and it seemed as if the rich, sun-drenched days would go on forever.

For three more weeks, early risers were greeted by a hot, radiant, golden sun. Everyone would have liked this state of affairs to continue, but knew in their hearts that this was only a gift, an offering from the gods to compensate them in some way for all those frightful, wet summers of the past few years.

The harvest was a record one with high yields and low moisture. The old-fashioned threshing machine, though now being overtaken by technology, continued to move from one farm to another, especially the small or medium farms, followed by most of the neighbouring farmers as they helped each other out. Paddy was of course in the middle of all the work, able to fill in at any of the dozen or more different jobs and do them better than anyone else. When the threshing came to his own place, his hospitality was as generous as ever.

Betty was not present, but there was some talk of overtime at the hospital. Meanwhile, Paddy did the work of two men, and drove his neighbours, with good-humoured jibes, to work just as hard as he did. Finally, near sunset, the last bag of grain was heaved into the store, and all departed to their own homes with a weary sense of relief.

That was a year when everything was saved, and bulging trailer loads of corn slowly made their way to the creamery, leaking a trickle of grain onto the roadside to the delight of rats and wood-pigeon alike. With the corn saved, those farmers who had availed of the combine harvester now called in the mechanical bailer, and set about saving the bailed straw, and day after day, young men and old men worked together, pitch-forking bales up onto trailers, quietly vying with each other to show their skills, and yet working as a team. When the load became very high, two men, working in unison, and with a graceful movement almost resembling a scene from a ballet, (or two hurlers stretching their *camáns* for the *sliotar*) forked and swung bales—in the last upward thrust using one hand each—to the very top of the load.

At last the work came to an end, and it was with a deep sense of satisfaction that the men made their way home, the dusk closing in around them as the evenings had become noticeably shorter.

The month had hardly come to an end when, like a gigantic shutter, black clouds moved across the sky and the wind picked up, creating miniature dust storms in the bone-dry fields before the temperature went down, and the torrential rains began. Farmers went around their yards and buildings, those with haystacks in haggards checking the tension of the ropes that held them together; those with barns and outbuildings casting a careful eye on their roofs of slates or corrugated iron.

It was around this time that people began to notice that Paddy and Betty were not to be seen together any more. Paddy still showed up at the creamery each morning with the milk in the horse and cart, but he was nearly always the first to arrive and the first to leave. He seemed pre-occupied and anxious to get his business over and done with, and didn't have time for small-talk.

Then word trickled out from the hospital. Betty Keogh was no longer there. The postman had a sister who worked in the hospital, and she said Betty had gone to England. Apparently she was going to work over there.

When the news went around the pub there wasn't a

single person who did not shake their head sympathetically when they heard it. It was quietly agreed that it would be better to say nothing about it. To Paddy, that is. Otherwise it was the main topic of conversation for several weeks.

They need not have worried about Paddy overhearing the gossip however, because as the days and weeks went by there was no sign of him at the pub. Callers to his house, on one pretext or another, who were always received cordially, noticed the Ford car abandoned behind the manure heap (it would stay there for evermore, changing colour like the seasons, from green to rusty red).

Various schemes were concocted to get Paddy back to his old life. A highly sought-after place in the weekly card game became vacant, a place for which many had waited for years. By general agreement it was offered to Paddy but he politely turned it down.

Then, his presence was urgently required on the inter-pub quiz team, "We'll be lost without you Paddy", But he smiled and shook his head. Nothing worked.

The days turned into years and the years into decades. Paddy's life revolved around the farm, the creamery shop, and weekly mass.

Many of his old friends gradually passed away and Paddy himself became something of a legend. Some old-timers remembered how he was the life and soul of any gathering in the pub in the old days, but most people forgot the circumstances which had caused him to shun most social activities. But his knowledge of farming and country lore brought both young and old to his house for advice or a chat. They were welcomed into the big, dark kitchen, cool in summer but warmed in winter by the huge fire, sometimes fed by long ash logs protruding across the concrete floor. There, he would listen patiently to his visitors' questions, whether they were about livestock or tillage, or, on occasion, personal matters, and in due course give his answers, most of which would be of a practical or common-sense nature.

Most of his younger visitors, including his niece Delia, who spent a good part of her summers on the farm, used to love hearing him talk about "the old days", and ploughing from dawn to dusk behind two strong and sometimes wayward horses— he was proud of the silver cups he had won at ploughing competitions. But all his visitors were surprised at his in-depth knowledge of current local happenings, considering that he was something of a recluse, and he particularly enjoyed retailing racy items of local gossip as he puffed on a Woodbine while staring at, and occasionally spitting into, the glowing logs.

Gradually, as he got older, he lost interest in farming but still saved the best hay in the area, which he kept for his neighbours.

There came a time when he began to dread the winters

and their long, dark, damp days. He particularly hated November;

"It's going nowhere," he used to say.

Although his relatives, and his niece in particular, visited when they could, the winter was lonely on the farm.

February is a month dreaded by the old. True, it is near the end of winter, and the first of February is sometimes referred to as the first day of spring, but it is a time when the old and the infirm are at a very low ebb. They have used up their small reserve of strength to carry them through the cold, gloomy days from November to the end of January.

One Sunday in early February, one of Paddy's neighbours called to bring him to Mass, as had been the custom for some years. Continued knocking at the door brought no response.

Another neighbour was called and after much knocking the door was forced open. At first there was no sign of Paddy. The neighbours walked slowly and carefully through the big kitchen calling his name. They passed into the dusty parlour, glancing at, but hardly seeing, the old family photographs on the wall, the tarnished silver cups on the sideboard.

"Paddy?"

"Are you awake Paddy?"

At last, when the smallest bedroom was entered he was found there, where he had died in his sleep.

The church was packed for the funeral. There were very few people in the area who did not know him or know of him. In the absence of anything else to say to express their genuine sorrow, the words 'end of an era' and, 'he was a gentleman' came into frequent use.

In the bitter wind a large crowd of relations, cousins, friends and acquaintances, gathered around the grave for the last prayers, but all were relieved when the parish priest, in fear of causing two or three more funerals, quickly brought the sad proceedings to an end.

Very soon the pub, two or three minutes down the road, was packed, and a warm and pleasant fug had established itself. The lady of the house, and her assistant, struggled to keep up with the orders shouted over the loud and merry chatter which seems to follow many funerals, as the mourners (other than the immediate family) unconsciously celebrate their own survival.

One of the mourners in the crowded pub that night was Paddy's niece Delia, now living in Dublin, and some weeks after the funeral, she was surprised to find that Paddy had left the farm to her. Delia decided she would keep the old farmhouse, for the time being at any rate, and let out the land. She took some holiday time due to her and moved down the country to do some cleaning up.

The building was cold and damp, but there was plenty of wood piled up in the corner of the kitchen and she decided to light the fire. She sat for twenty minutes or so, feeding the small flames, and occasionally operating the blower, until she had a good blaze going, and then went to have a look at the rest of the house.

Very little of the contents were worth saving. Whatever had escaped the damp had been destroyed by woodworm.

Delia kept Paddy's little silver cups, though the silver gilt had all but gone. The dark, gloomy photographs too, even though she was unsure of the identity of the gaunt, worn people in them, she carefully packed away.

The old sideboard was made of black oak and had resisted both damp and wood beetle. In its lower drawers were a few bottles half full of assorted liquids. In most cases mice had eaten the labels for the glue in them. In the top drawer there was an assortment of candle stubs, old Christmas cards, safety pins and a few buttons. Delia decided that the best thing to do was to tip the lot into the fire, but as she did so, she found a small package of letters. Six of them had Irish stamps and had been addressed, in Paddy's distinctive clear hand, to a Miss Betty Keogh, SRN, at different hospitals in the Manchester area. They had all been posted within a period of three weeks or so but all had been returned unopened and officially stamped "Unknown at this Address". Hardly thinking, Delia threw them on the fire.

The remaining envelope was addressed to Paddy. It had an English stamp and a Manchester postmark with a date which preceded the other six letters. It contained a single sheet of notepaper, and, as Delia looked at the tidy, feminine writing she suddenly realised that it, along with the other letters which were now unfortunately burning in the fire, was the answer to Paddy's mysterious withdrawal to a hermit-like lifestyle.

The letter was dated but the writer had omitted the address. The small, careful handwriting said;

"Dear Paddy,

I've got the position ! I'm really thrilled !

I'm starting immediately. Thanks for the lovely time we had during the summer. I'll never forget it.

Please write as soon as you can.

Love,   Betty

THE PAPER TIDE

Regent's Terrace is a pretty little row of houses lining the side of a steep hill opposite the old city hospital. Just six houses in all, built in the regency period before the reign of Queen Victoria, a touch of elegance inserted amongst the plain, grey houses which occupied most of the street.

The hill at that point is steep and the architect had contrived to produce a sort of split level effect. The ground floor served in fact as a basement. Above it, the main part of each house was set back some ten or twelve feet from the street, and residents and visitors were prevented from tumbling into the roadway by a pleasant cast-iron railing which ran along the top of the basement level of all six houses. However, the height of the basements diminished as the hill rose so that the basement of the sixth house was a very cramped affair indeed.

Most of the owners or residents had placed earthenware pots and assorted containers of geraniums and other flowers about their front doors, and access to this charming upper terrace was gained via a series of limestone steps at the upper end of the row of houses.

At the basement level of each house a plain, anonymous door led onto the street, but on the upper level the front of each house consisted of a fine front door with a Georgian style fanlight and multi-paned sash windows at each side.

So it was to one of these houses that James, a young estate agent, came, in the spring of the year, to determine its value, at the request of Mr.Rothwell, the solicitor. As a matter of fact, Mr. Rothwell hadn't been particularly keen for James to actually visit the house, and had told him so when he arrived to pick up the keys.

"Can you not tell the value from recent sales in the area?" he inquired, squinting one eye and clamping his jaw in a little way he had.

"No" said James, "I prefer to actually see the inside from top to bottom. You never know if the place is riddled with dry-rot or rising damp, or indeed if the place has been maintained like a palace."

"Very well," said the solicitor, with a sigh, "I'll make the necessary arrangements, but don't use the key unless you have to."

It appeared, as James gathered from subsequent comments made by the solicitor, that the current resident of the house was not the owner, but had been a tenant for many years. Unfortunately, the relationship between the tenant, a retired naval officer, and the owners (distant relatives) had become strained, and had led to a situation where the tenant felt himself to be under siege and now rejected any attempts on the part of the owners to gain admittance. Hence the reluctance on the part of the solicitor to encourage the valuer to attempt to enter the building.

However, James had always been fascinated by this little terrace of houses—one rarely came up for sale—and in due course, dressed in his best suit, he arrived at Regent's Terrace and strode up the steps and along to the front door of the house. Here he surreptitiously polished the tops of his shoes on the back of his trouser legs, held his canvas-backed, black notebook to his breast, and lifted the heavy knocker.

To say he was not a little nervous would be a lie. He had heard that the old gentleman had been a champion boxer in his navy days, and it was said that he still "worked out." Indeed, in recent times he had put the run on a pair of muggers who had accosted him on his way home from the local pub. One of the gurriers was said to be taking a case against him for knocking out two of his teeth.

The knocker came in heavy contact with the door and

the boom echoed in the hall beyond. Silence followed.

James waited for a minute or so and then raised the knocker and let it fall again. Once more, silence.

He thought for a moment, and then retraced his steps into the street until he came to the basement door. Here was a smaller knocker, which he rattled several times. To his surprise the door opened immediately, and the narrow opening was filled by the somewhat menacing presence of a large elderly man dressed in black trousers and a vest. The trousers were made of a heavy material much used by the manufacturers of service uniforms. The vest, James thought, was probably common or garden civilian issue, and had originally been white, but sometime in its long life, had taken on a shade of green.

"Yes?" said the tenant.

"Ahem, ah, good morning, ah, command-em, ah, Mr. Roche " James stuttered, "I've come to value the house for insurance purposes—has Mr.Rothwell been in touch?"

"Oh, him" Mr. Roche furrowed his brows which were black and incredibly bushy. He breathed heavily for a moment or two, staring suspiciously at James.

"What do you have to do?" he said.

"I have to examine the house, mm, from top to bottom if possible," said James, running the tip of his tongue along his upper lip.

Mr. Roche gave a peculiar little cough, muttered something about "highly inconvenient, so it is" and then said loudly;

"Well, you had betther come in then."

He turned around and walked heavily into the gloom of the basement. James followed him, glancing from left to right while opening his notebook and taking out his pen.

On each side of the corridor were small rooms, originally pantries, sculleries and the like, now disused apart from a lavatory whose rusty cistern overflowed continuously. James clicked on the light in the lavatory, noting the old-fashioned pull-chain. High on the wall beside the cistern, a grubby hand had pressed against the grey plaster many times, leaving the blurred impression of outspread fingers.

They came to a narrow staircase, and as Mr. Roche began to clump up them, one step at a time, coughing as he did so, James glanced into a room on his right. It had once been a bathroom but was now covered in dust and grime. A large, cast-iron bath stood in the centre of the room. It was full to the very brim with thick, slimy, green water. For some reason it looked ominous. James could hear a heavy "Drip, drip, drip," somewhere in the background. He blinked and unconsciously scribbled "bath, green water" in his notebook.

Mr. Roche was waiting for him at the top of the flight of stairs. He turned and James followed him into the large front room—but not very far. The room was knee-deep in paper of all kinds. Mainly newspapers, but also bills, statements, shopping lists, junk mail, old photos, newspaper cuttings, and, to an amazing extent, squares of cardboard used by commercial laundries for shirts. Here and there assorted undergarments had been cast in little heaps.

Mr. Roche cleared his throat and muttered something about not having had time to go to what he called "the landry."

James busied himself scribbling details of the room, and noted that, in a little oasis on the mantelpiece, there were three or four old photographs, flanked on one side by a pair of brass shell casings (from a naval gun he presumed), and on the other by a large, discoloured and tarnished silver cup. One photo showed a handsome young man, possibly Roche, dressed in boxing gear and holding a cup—the one on the mantelpiece. The others were of groups of young naval officers.

The dining room was much the same. A cracked mahogany table with one or two chairs surrounded by snowdrifts of paper.

They passed the tiny kitchen and James caught a glimpse of an ancient electric cooker, black with burnt grease.

Mr. Roche dismissed the kitchen with a priestly wave of his hand and headed for the hall and the staircase, which had a row of carved wooden banister railings all the way up to the top. James noticed that, from where they started at ground level in the hall, to a level determined by the height of the raised hand of a standing, elderly, retired naval officer, the banisters were absolutely crammed with rolled or folded newspapers, placed there individually it would seem, over a long period of time.

By the time they reached the first floor Mr. Roche was breathing heavily. The two bedrooms on this floor had also been invaded by paper, but not to such an immobilising effect as on the floor below. In one of the bedrooms Mr. Roche maintained an island which contained his bed and, on one side of it, a small bedside table crammed with medications, lucozade, tea-cups, tissues, Q-tips and all the other minutiae of his life. On the other side a stack of yellowing paperback books teetered precariously.

Finally there was the attic, reached by a narrow set of steps which Mr. Roche pointed out to James before he himself began to descend to the ground floor. James carefully tiptoed up the little steps and glanced at the two rather pokey, empty rooms under the slanting roof. The paper tide had not reached here he noticed.

When he returned to the ground floor he found that Mr. Roche seemed to have retired to the little kitchen. The rattle of pots and pans came from the half open door.

James tapped on it and Mr. Roche's cross, red face appeared.

"Yes, yes, yes, what is it now ?" he snapped.
James felt his own face turn red as he stuttered,
"I'm sorry Mr. Roche, I just wanted to thank you for letting me see the house."
Mr. Roche looked puzzled for a moment, then the great creases in his face relaxed, and the bushy eyebrows returned to their normal position as he looked at James as if for the first time.

"Oh yes, that's right, that's right," he whispered, "Of course I'll be cleanin' it all up any day now."

James returned to his office, and, within a few days had forgotten all about Mr. Roche and his newspapers.

About five months later, he received a phone call from Mr.Rothwell, who informed him that Mr. Roche had passed away, found dead in his bed apparently. Could James please get details ready for a Sale-By-

Auction notice as soon as possible?

"Of course," said James, "I'll pop over tomorrow and give the place a quick look over."

James heard a slight clicking on the phone line which he knew was Mr.Rothwell clamping his jaw in that way he had.

"Sure, you were there only a few months ago" said the solicitor.

"That's true, but you know the way I like to check things." said James.

"Oh very well then, but be sure to have it in this week's paper," said the solicitor as he hung up.

James could have prepared the details from the notes of his previous visit but he was still curious about the house, and so, the next morning, he drove over to Regent's Terrace. A Yale key, shiny and brassy with age and use, had been provided by the solicitor and fitted smoothly into the lock of the basement door.

James pushed the door open and stood there for a moment, getting used to the dim light and testing the various smells that presented themselves. Damp was one, and possibly dry rot was another. But a third smell overcame the other two. It was a deep and pervading smell of decay.

He felt for a light switch and eventually found one that turned on a weak bulb in the stairwell. He glanced around and into the small chambers that were on each side of the gloomy passage. He noted that the bathroom with the bath full of green liquid had not changed. The same drip he remembered from his last visit, continued to keep perfect time in seconds.

He went forward to the stairs and climbed to the hall above.

The paper tide had not gone out, he mused. In fact there seemed to be even more paper. The sitting room at the front of the house was awash with the stuff, the old newspapers and laundry packaging now covered with a dressing of old bills, prescriptions and shopping lists, seemingly emptied out of the drawers of a tilting sideboard.

The silver cup and the brass shell casings had disappeared. The old photographs remained.

James made his way up the stairs, his knees brushing the numerous newspapers jammed in the banisters. The bedrooms were also full of paper, and not a bed to be seen.

Out on the landing again, he glanced upwards and noticed that a light appeared to be on in the attic.

He carefully mounted the steep steps until his eyes

became level with the attic floor. The small room contained an iron bedstead with a mattress on it, and a simple bedside table littered with assorted bottles and packets. Vick's Night Nurse, Rennies tablets, Lemsip, Coleman's Mustard.

An old-fashioned lamp-socket with a pull-switch hung from the rafters over the bed. That's where the light was coming from. Oddly, there was not a scrap of paper to be seen.

He hauled himself up into the small room, crouching a little to avoid the rafters, and wondering how Mr. Roche managed it. He stood on something which slipped on the floor, causing him to fall face down on the small bed. To his horror the mattress was still warm, and had an unpleasant smell.

He recoiled from it in shock. His brain told him to pull himself together—the hanging lamp had kept the bed warm. He felt around on the floor for the thing that had caused him to slip and picked it up. It was a dental plate—Mr. Roche's dental plate in fact. He dropped it on the side table and involuntarily wiped his hand on his trouser leg, before scrambling down the steps and on down the stairs. It took him about ten seconds to get from the attic to his car.

He seemed to lose interest in the house after that, always getting his brash young assistant to show the property to prospective clients. The assistant thought the house was hilarious and loved showing it—especially to nervous young women.

Shortly before the auction, the owners had the house cleaned from top to bottom. Every scrap of paper and mite of dust was removed, the windows were cleaned, the old cooker dumped, and a coat of paint applied to every room.

Still, the house did not make the reserve price at auction, and took a long time to sell by private treaty. But the assistant eventually found a 'victim'(as he liked to refer to buyers) and introduced him to James in the hall of the house when final terms of the sale were being agreed.

The new resident turned out to be an elderly bachelor who had been something of an athlete in his day. A tall, distinguished-looking man, he stood with his back to the staircase, a pipe in one hand and, tucked under his arm, a folded copy of the *Irish Times.*

When James offered him a copy of the Terms of Sale, he took the newspaper from under his arm, looked around, and with an "Ah!" of satisfaction, tucked it between the banisters on the stairs.

THE BARBECUE

Dooley sat on the small single bed and polished his battered brogues. After his shower he had put on his Irish Rugby Team shirt and a pair of jeans—his standard outfit for barbecues. Now he slipped on his shoes and went out to the corridor.

"Are you ready?" he shouted.

"I'm coming" his wife Mary shouted from the master bedroom. He headed out to the car, reflecting briefly on the current state of their marriage.

He had moved into the spare bedroom a few weeks ago in a fit of defiance. Now he found it hard to go back to the matrimonial bed. It wasn't an ideal situation he admitted to himself. Still, it had its good points. He slept very well. That is, on the nights when he wasn't wide awake worrying about the future.

He climbed into the car and started the engine. The passenger door opened and Mary climbed in, bringing with her a waft of perfume. She was nicely made up he noted, even though her face was utterly and completely expressionless, like the face of a mannequin in an up-market shop window.

Dooley put the car in gear and drove off. One of his friends, Ross, was having the barbecue, just a couple of miles away.

Ross was having his own marital problems, but the two wives seemed to get along fine, probably comparing notes on the iniquities of men thought Dooley to himself.

The narrow country road wound its way between high ditches of lichen-covered stones and grassy sods. Between the road and the ditch on each side there was a drain where water bubbled and gullied along. They met one car and pulled in to let it pass, waving automatically to the driver, whom, though unseen behind the muddy windscreen, they probably knew, this being such a remote area.

At a crossroads stood a small cottage. The owner was reputed to be a writer but was almost never there. Two chained dogs sat in the drive. One was a Doberman and the other was a larger dog, a strange cross between a Labrador and something like a Rhodesian ridge-back. Usually both of them growled ferociously whenever anyone passed by, the large mongrel being the most frightening of the two, with it's bright red hair standing on end along it's spine.

As the car paused at the crossroads, Dooley leaned out the window.

"Hello boys" he said, and was immediately taken aback when the two dogs rushed down the drive towards him growling fiercely. The big mongrel was spitting foam. They were both brought to an abrupt standstill when the chains ran out of slack.

Dooley muttered "Phew!" and pressed the accelerator.

"Serves you right," said Mary.

A few minutes later they arrived at the Ross house, a converted farm building on several acres which had been beautifully landscaped and planted with trees and shrubs. Dooley could see Ross some distance away from the house, setting up trestle tables. He parked the car outside the house and walked over to him. (Mary had headed straight for the kitchen where Sheelagh, Ross's wife, was presumably preparing food).

Ross was pleased to see Dooley.

"Ah, the very man. I'm glad you came early; you can give me a hand with the wine and stuff—here, you might as well have a glass while you're at it."

He handed Dooley a large glass of deep red wine.

And that was the beginning, Dooley thought to himself afterwards.

He set to with enthusiasm, erecting tables and chairs, opening bottles of wine, and topping up his and Ross's glasses frequently—"we have to test it you know!" while Ross told him the most outrageous jokes.

Guests were slow to arrive. A lot of them were tucking into a foundation down at the pub. Mary and Sheelagh appeared for a while but soon disappeared into the house, rubbing the goose pimples from their arms as the sun began to go down.

Dooley was by now in what he would call "good form". He and Ross had opened and "tested" a sufficient number of wine bottles and now they began to set up the music system. A sheltered area by the orchard wall had been designated "the dance area" and soon one or two couples were moving around. As more people arrived the hub-hub of conversation rose and the music was turned up to compensate.

Ross introduced Dooley to a woman he did business with. She was fortyish, blonde, quite attractive, and dressed in skin-tight jeans and a silky blouse. She seemed to be by herself and was enjoying her drink. She enthusiastically accepted Dooley's invitation to dance.

The "dance-floor" was only rough ground by the

orchard wall but soon the two of them were lurching around like they had known each other forever. When the slow music came on they clung to each other like limpets. Her mouth was pleasantly near his ear whispering sweet nothings to his grunts of acknowledgement. He had his arms around her waist and her arms were around his neck.

This is kind of cosy thought Dooley to himself, not really sure where the business was going to end up, but enjoying thinking of the possibilities.

Then she said "Oh-oh!"

"What is it? said Dooley.

"Here comes fuck-face." she said in a hard voice. Taken aback by the language, Doyle turned around and looked towards the house. A man was walking slowly up the path towards the barbecue area. A big, burly, ugly man. He wore a black leather jacket, black shirt and black trousers. He was heavily built and his head was shaven. He was also cross-eyed.

"And who exactly is fuck-face?" asked Dooley, still watching the approaching man. She had dropped her arms and he also adopted a more neutral dancing posture.

"He's my husband," said the blonde, looking Dooley up and down as if wondering whether he might be the champion who would free her from this monster. She quickly came to the conclusion that he wasn't.

"See ya" she said, and walked away.

"See ya" said Dooley out loud (and "Christ!" under his breath).

He walked over to where the wine was and helped himself to a large glass. Then he joined Ross and a few others scraping the bottom of the joke barrel.

He saw Mary once or twice, when she and Sheelagh ventured out to the barbecue for a plateful of black sausage and black steak. But by then the singing had begun and he was in full flight.

A couple of hours passed like fifteen minutes. By now, most of the revellers had gone home and Dooley's shirt was becoming damp with dew. He and Ross were flaked out in a pair of deckchairs, a half tumbler of port in their hands. Both of them were pissed.

"Look here ol' chap" said Dooley in a peculiar, army officer accent, which for some reason he sometimes assumed when he was drunk;

"I shall have to head back to barracks now. I will get my lady to drive me."   He belched loudly.

"I say Dooley" said Ross, who had also assumed an army alter ego. "I'm afraid your missus has gone home long ago—she took the car don't ya know. But not to worry, ol' chap, we'll find a billet for you here".

But Dooley was quite put out by this state of affairs. He would not put "the lady of the house" to any inconvenience, he stated ponderously, but would march home. Ross did his best to persuade him to stay but Dooley was adamant. In his warped and alcohol-sodden mind he saw himself marching strongly off up the country road, an ash stick under one arm, the other arm swinging in a military fashion.

Ross staggered into the house to find a torch to give him but when he came out Dooley had gone.

Ross slowly made his way back into the house and five minutes later he lay snoring on the living room sofa.

Dooley, meanwhile, was finding that it was not so easy to 'march' home, with a load of drink on board and in the almost pitch dark. Soon his gait became that of a very old and blind man—a drunk blind man— hands feeling out before him and beside him, legs apart and each foot being placed tentatively and uncertainly in front of the other.

After five hundred yards he sunk his right foot in the mucky drain beside the road. He swore loudly as he pulled it out, and stamped it several times to get rid of the wet mud. He carried on cautiously and after another five hundred yards sank his left foot in a very wet and deep drain. He was now deeply regretting his decision to 'march' home.

Then, in the distance, he saw a light. Although it wobbled a bit in his eyes it didn't grow any bigger or smaller so he reckoned it was stationary. Striving to focus his vision, he peered through the dark, using the light as a guide, and staggered on, singing Colonel Bogey's March.

Suddenly, he knew where he was. It was the writer's cottage. Just the outside light was on, there was no car parked outside, and there seemed to be no one in the house.

Dooley stood at the open gate and leaned against a tree to steady himself. Now, where are those bloody dogs, he thought. His answer was a snarl as the Doberman appeared out of nowhere and began curling his lip over fangs which shone in the light from the gate lamp. A louder snarl came from the big mongrel, which now appeared on the road side of the open gate.

Christ! thought Dooley, they're not on chains.

At that moment he staggered, tripped over something, and fell to his knees on the tarmacadam drive.

The dogs looked on, momentarily puzzled.

At this stage Doyle was more pissed-off than scared. He suddenly let out a roar like an angry wolf and went for the dogs on his hands and knees, snarling. Their reaction was immediate. They both dropped to the ground, turned over on their backs and waggled their paws in the air. The mongrel ridge-back did her best to imitate a human smile, drawing her lips back to show her shiny teeth.

"Well, ye pair of imposters" said Dooley, immediately reaching out and tickling the two dogs and rolling over on his own back.

He lay there, with his two new friends, laughing quietly and admiring the stars which were starting to fade as the summer dawn began to seep over the horizon.

He could never remember quite how he made it home but he did. He vaguely remembered falling into his little bed in his damp clothes and after that— oblivion.

The sun was streaming through a crack in the curtains when something awoke him suddenly. He was lying on his side facing the wall but he knew someone was in bed with him. He felt very disoriented, nauseous. His tongue was stuck to the roof of his mouth.

He desperately tried to gather his memory. Have I done something awful he thought, vague memories of the blonde and fuck-face passing through his mind. No, no, I couldn't have he thought.

Unless……. could it be Mary, he thought, coming to make up?

At that moment a warm tongue tickled his ear.

He turned around with a bleary smile.

But it wasn't Mary — or the blonde.

It was a very happy and contented, mongrel Rhodesian ridge-back.

THE GREAT MAN

Close contact with other people's smelly bodies had never been Kevin's favourite thing. Especially when, during his boarding school days, those smelly bodies belonged to his fellow students and were covered in mud, as they usually were on the rugby field.

All right, so he wasn't heavy enough to be a forward anyway so that would keep him out of the scrum. What about the backs, or even the wing?.......Mm, true.. but there was only one problem.

From birth Kevin had been equipped with the finest set of butterfingers known to man. He couldn't catch a ball, any ball, big, small, round or oblong, for love nor money.

His abilities, or lack of them, were quickly and silently assessed by the school coach and, possibly as a way of postponing the inevitable, he was given the position of full back.

At first he gloried in his lonely position, dancing up

55

and down and running on the spot to keep warm, his shorts pristine white compared to those of all the other members of his team.

He remembered seeing the full-back of one of the senior Dublin teams jogging up and down near the goal posts while his team mates hammered the opposition miles away down the other end of the pitch. A group of girls stayed at the full-back's end however, linking arms with each other, admiring his short white pants and his long brown muscular thighs, and giggling into their school scarves.

Kevin had to admit that his own thighs were neither muscular nor brown. Skinny and blue would be a better description, with goose pimples added for effect. He feverishly rubbed his hands together to improve the circulation.

For the first game or two he got away with it. His team was better than their opponents and he never had to touch the ball. In fact he made a virtue of keeping a huge space between himself and his team mates so that a ball never came his way.

He soon began to believe that he wasn't a bad full back, and in fact, that a time would come when he would rescue the team from near disaster.

He rehearsed the moment in his mind. A fantastically

high ball dropping like a stone to be trapped in his arms and the pit of his stomach, followed immediately by a great clearing kick to touch, and a roar from the small crowd of fellow students.

Or perhaps a loose ball, bouncing threateningly towards the corner. An incredible sprint, a brilliant scoop, and a flick of the boot to touch before being bowled over by the enemy. This would, perhaps, be followed by the ministrations of an anxious coach with the First Aid kit, and a limping walk (aided by his comrades) to the changing rooms; accompanied by a verse of "Old Soldiers Never Die" from the sidelines, and some hand-clapping from his team mates.

If only. But alas, it was not to be. When they met a better team everything went wrong. He allowed the fantastically high ball to bounce and found himself grasping thin air while one of the other team stole a try. As for the bouncing loose ball, he never touched it, but instead accidentally tripped a team mate who might have saved it.

After that, the ball seemed to seek him out no matter where he positioned himself, and then evade his desperate fingers. He prayed for the final whistle but the clock seemed to go into slow motion while all his inadequacies were exposed. He tried to convince himself that it was only partly his fault that it was one of the worst defeats his team had ever experienced.

The next day the coach, in a somewhat restrained but kindly tone, suggested that he might join the soccer club.

The soccer club comprised of two types of players, in roughly equal proportions. One half were soccer fanatics, the other half were rugby rejects, eccentrics, and people who hated any type of sports but had to "tog out" under school standing orders.

A playing pitch was grudgingly given over to them, although it was on boggy land, and in winter contained sheets of water.

Kevin didn't do terribly well here either, although the butterfinger problem had not spread entirely to his toes. He was able, occasionally, to produce what was disparagingly referred to by the real soccer players as a 'toedriver,' and send the ball, bouncing like a dambuster's bomb, across the pools of rainwater in the general direction of the goal. In truth, his heart was not in it, and he spent an inordinate amount of time on the sidelines repairing broken bootlaces and the like.

The school years went by, college went by, and soon his disastrous school sports days were but a distant, distasteful memory stored in the less frequented parts of his mind.

He had discovered several other more interesting

pastimes, including drinking beer, chasing girls, and dancing. Drinking beer was by far the most important and soon he was part of a small group of young men who met every Friday and Saturday night, to consume the black gold, crack jokes, talk rubbish, and, as the night went on, sing Irish songs.

He became great friends with Seamus, a handsome, dark-haired, athletic young man who hadn't a note in his head but loved a good joke. His great laugh was a joy to hear, so he was kept well supplied with stories by his friends. On rare occasions, when they were not talking about epoch-making drinking sessions, girls, or cars, the conversation drifted into the area of sports, and Kevin learned that Seamus had been a very well-known and promising hurler at Junior level, but had completely dropped the sport when he went to university.

One summer evening Kevin and Seamus were having a pint in one of their favourite drinking haunts; a small hotel near the coast. Although the night was still a pup, there was quite a large gathering in the comfortable lounge, and the two of them had ensconced themselves on one of a pair of sofas in the centre of the room.

As they were coming to the end of their first pint, a tall, weather-beaten man wearing a pinstriped suit, approached and sat down opposite them.

"By God is it you Seamus" he said, placing his pint of

Guinness on the table with one hand and loosening his double-breasted suit jacket with the other. He was probably about sixty but looked lean and fit.

"How are ye Paddy" said Seamus, shaking his hand. Then, looking at his friend he said,

" Kevin, this is Paddy O'Toole, you know, captain of the county team which won the All-Ireland a few years back."

Charlie smiled and grasped the huge hand, muttering "Of course, of course," although the name was only vaguely familiar to him.

O'Toole focused his attention on Seamus.

"Well, Seamus, I must say I had great hopes for ye— what a waste of talent—begob, we might have won the All-Ireland again!"

Seamus just threw back his head and roared with laughter. Faces turned from the bar.

"And what team did this man play for?" said the great man, turning to Kevin, who was forced to admit that not only did he not play for any team but had never taken a hurley or a *sliothar* in his hand.

"By God, and you call yourself an Irishman?" said O'Toole, shaking his head from side to side—"any young man who has never taken up a hurley or a football cannot call himself a true Irishman."

He put his hand on his hip and looked at Kevin with a kind of "who-let-him-in" expression.

Kevin could only look back with a cross between a weak smile and a grimace on his face; the Great Man's voice had been loud and Kevin was conscious of several people in the bar listening to the conversation.

And then something came over Kevin. His facial expression became deeply serious. He glanced at Seamus and muttered "Same again Seamus?" and then began to rise, slowly, very, very slowly, from the sofa. He gritted his teeth and his knuckles became white as he assumed a stooped, almost upright position. One of his legs hung in a strange crooked way behind him, the foot jutting out at an odd angle.

Again gritting his teeth and breathing heavily, he reached down with two hands and dragged the wretched limb forward some ten inches in the direction of the bar.

A pause followed, accompanied by a gasp for breath. Then the "good leg" hopped forward one pace. Again, the hands reached painfully down and dragged the palsied limb forward. Briefly, from the corner of his eye, Kevin saw the Great Man staring at him, his face locked in surprise.

A few more, seemingly agonising steps, and he had

reached the bar counter. He laid his elbows on it and slowly turned around.

The Great Man had gone, his pint abandoned.

Seamus sat with his glass held frozen near his mouth, which was half open, a look of total incredulity across his face. Then his head went back, his mouth opened wider, and a gale of laughter filled the room.

THE VIGIL

It was a modern church, built of some kind of mass concrete, and yet the interior had the echoing solemnity that he associated with all churches, temples and houses of God.

The main altar was situated in the centre of the building, and all around it, pews descended in a gentle slope. It was a kind of theatre in the round, but a theatre devoted to the sacrifice of the mass.

Apart from a huge slab of stained glass in an abstract design, which wrapped itself half way around the building, the structure was devoid of any form of bright decoration. Instead, the drab, gray concrete of its construction, already twenty years old, stood ready to receive the patination of the next one hundred years.

The building was redolent with the atmosphere of worship and devotion; a comforting mixture of burnt candle-wax, floor polish and incense.

And here it was that Ryan, enthusiastic agnostic and

half-hearted atheist, forced-fed with religion during his boarding school days, came to visit the remains of his father, now in an oak coffin before the altar, on the eve of his funeral.

In spite of his long absence from places of worship, Ryan automatically dipped his finger in the holy water font and blessed himself before moving up the aisle. The church appeared to be empty and the lighting was very dim. A sanctuary light glowed in the dark shadow of the main altar, but a small cluster of prayer candles near the coffin provided most of the light.

His polished shoes clattered loudly on the parquet floor as he walked slowly past the rows of pews.

As he reached the halfway point, his nostrils drew his attention to a dim area near a large radiator. An elderly tramp sat there, arms folded, his head on his chest, his huge frame made even bigger by the numerous garments he wore. Known to everyone as Fortycoats, he spent a considerable part of his winter days and evenings (when he had finished 'me rounds' as he used to say), in this position. On the rather rare occasions when Ryan attended mass, he had noticed that an almost perfect circle of empty pews surrounded Fortycoats, even when the church was packed. But on this occasion, the presence of Fortycoats barely registered as he continued his walk up the aisle.

At the front pew he paused and genuflected slowly, before moving in and assuming a half sitting, half kneeling position, his eyes on the coffin in front of him.

His father would have been buried already were it not for the delay requested by Ryan's sister, who was at that moment somewhere over the Atlantic, en route from California.

It had all been so horrendously, so cruelly, sudden. There had been no time or opportunity for words of love, of apology, of regret, of thanks. The circumstances would bother and trouble him for a long time afterwards.

Just three days ago, having taken the afternoon off from work, he had received a phone call from his office. It had been his father, who had asked, querulously and plaintively;

"Where are you? I dropped in to see you."

Ryan had made some excuse, not noticing the anxiety in his father's voice. An hour later, his secretary phoned to say that his father had collapsed while walking up the town.

An old friend of his father's had just happened to be nearby and had immediately informed the office.

As Ryan's secretary spoke nervously on the phone, he could hear a siren in the background, and, as his office was on the main route to the hospital he had often wondered later if it had been the ambulance carrying his father.

Hurriedly, he packed his wife and two children into the car and drove as fast as he could to the hospital. There seemed to be some confusion when he arrived. A young nurse, nervous and reluctant to tell him anything, had ushered him into the presence of a doctor, who, assuming he knew the worst, had simply said,

"Ah yes Mr. Ryan; your father was dead on arrival, there was nothing we could do."

Ryan remembered giving a dazed nod, and then returning to the car, driving slowly, like a robot, to the home of his mother, a cheerful sixty-two year-old who thought she was still forty-two, and making her sit down so that he could give her the worst news she would ever hear in her life.

Ryan sighed. Giving her the news had been like beating some innocent poor creature with a club, while she cried and screamed, over and over,
"No! no! no!"
He would never forget it. Now, half seated in the pew, his hands clasped before him, he shook the memory from his mind, and squeezed his eyes shut. Surprisingly, they were quite dry, the contact between eye-lids and eyes feeling rough and salty. He had no tears left he

supposed, or maybe he was just too tired and hung-over to find tears, although there had been plenty of tears the night before.

Not however, when he greeted the many friends and relations who had come to the house. Not when he pressed whisky and sherry on them. Not when jokes were told of bygone days. Not when relations from the midlands whom he had not seen for twenty years, and probably would not see for another twenty, shook his hand fiercely.

But every now and then, when he left the babble of voices and the clouds of cigarette smoke, and ran upstairs to see his mother, lying in a state of shock on her bed— *their* bed— a damp facecloth on her forehead and an old jumper of his father's clutched tightly in her arms, the tears flowed. A long hug, his tears mingling with those of his mother, and then it was down the stairs again with a forced smile for the visiting mourners. How strange, that within minutes of returning to the sitting room, he could be laughing out loud at some re-telling of an old family yarn…

Ryan stared at the little group of candles on the brass stand in front of him. Some were sputtering and flaring as their short lives came to an end. The image blurred as Ryan thought again of his father and the relationship between them.

His father had been a good man, there was no doubt about that. As a young man he had found a company willing to take him on during the great depression of the 'Thirties, and had stayed with them for all of his working life. He rose slowly in the ranks until he was office manager and company secretary. He was strict and yet kindly with those under him. Many of those he trained went on to better things in bigger companies but never forgot their days under his father.

Two of them were at the house last night, big shots now of course, joking about how his father insisted on the petty cash being balanced to the last penny every Friday, otherwise, whoever was in charge of it for that week had to make up any discrepancy out of their own pay.

Then there was the time when he reminded the chairman that he owed the petty cash forty pounds. The chairman was not best pleased and the incident possibly cost his father a directorship.

And then, over the years, his father had devoted himself to community organisations, rotary, fundraisers, past pupils' unions and the like.

He attended 10.30 Mass every Sunday without fail, and at home, insisted on the Rosary being said every day after tea until the children were big enough to rebel and had found ways of sneaking out of the house.

Sadly, father and eldest son rarely saw eye to eye. The gap between a young man of the Depression and a young man of the Rock 'n' Roll era is mighty wide. Drainpipe trousers were frowned upon, suede shoes were frowned upon, and just about everything else, it seemed to the young Ryan, including staying out late and drinking beer at the age of seventeen.

Later, Ryan went away to university, and then travel and work overseas seemed to widen the gap between them. Nevertheless, in the last few years, since he had returned to his home town, they had begun to move closer. His father had mellowed with the years, or was it that Ryan's own current experiences of some of the trials of fatherhood had created common ground?

His thoughts wandered further back in time, to his childhood; capturing for a moment the scene on a typical sunny Saturday in the 'Sixties, when he, his brothers and sister, grandmother and parents, had all crammed into the small Ford car and headed to their favourite beach, a sandy cove far from any amusement arcades and much favoured by parents with young children. His father seemed all-powerful in that memory, towering over him, his arms folded on his suntanned chest, asking him was he going to come in for a swimming lesson.

Unfortunately, his father was an enthusiastic believer

in the sink or swim school and, with a roar of laughter, would grab any of his children who were foolish enough to get within range, and throw them out into the sea, from where they would be forced to doggy-paddle frantically, spluttering, to the shore. After one such episode, his seven-year-old younger brother had run up the beach and from a safe distance had roared at his father,

"You dirty eejit!" to the slightly shocked amusement of all the other families picnicking on the strand...

A shuffling noise echoed from the back of the dark, empty church. It drew nearer, accompanied by a strong odour, and stopped at his pew. Ryan hardly noticed, his mind still occupied with images of sandcastles, gritty sandwiches and his father furiously pumping an unco-operative Primus stove.

And then the smell hit him. He looked up and saw the red, bristly face of Fortycoats. The tramp nodded to him and then nodded in the direction of the coffin before muttering something in a deep guttural tone. Ryan could not understand what he had said, but was pleased that the old codger had offered his sympathy. He smiled and nodded his thanks. The tramp hesitated, then turned and moved a few feet down the aisle.

Ryan stared at the coffin. When he was a child, his parents went to the cinema three times a week. It was before television, and the cinema changed the feature film every two days. The children were allowed go to the matinee every Saturday afternoon, but when his mother had a cold or was unable to go, his father would turn to him and gravely ask him:

"Would you like to go to the pictures?" (he hated going alone). Needless to say, young Ryan would jump at the opportunity. How he loved being with his father among all the 'grown-ups' in the cinema, sharing a bag of Foxes' Glacier Mints!

Ryan was aware that the tramp had moved up to him again and was asking him a question, but he could not make out what it was. Holding his breath, Ryan put his face closer to the tramp's and said,

"Pardon?"

The tramp sighed, and with more than a hint of impatience said, very loudly indeed,

"CAN I HAVE HIS CLOTHES?"

Ryan gently waved him away, smiling half-bitterly to himself. Isn't that just typical he thought, although typical of what he didn't quite know.

At the same time a part of him felt, somehow, cheated out of his lone 'vigil'.

Then he smiled. On the other hand, he thought, Dad,

for all his solemnity, would have found the incident highly amusing— maybe he does in fact!

He sighed and sat back in the pew, his hands falling to his sides on the seat.

He glanced once more at the coffin. He took a deep breathe, exhaled, stood up, and walked slowly down the aisle and out of the church.

LOOKING GOOD

Ryder was a man who liked to look good.   He liked to be noticed—especially by women—as he made his way through life.

In his youth this had not been a problem. A memory from his teenage days often came back to him. In it, he had entered the unlit members' room of the local tennis club, a corrugated iron shack, late one summer night and found, in the dark, some of his teenage pals playing spin-the-bottle. As he stood there, a black shadow framed in the doorway, there were shouts of,

"Who is it ?" and "Go away!".

Then he heard Betty Wynn say in a loud voice,

"I'd recognise those square shoulders anywhere, that's Michael Ryder."

Betty Wynn was one of the most attractive girls in the club, and Ryder never quite forgot that insignificant little scene, in spite of the fact that he never managed to date her, and she soon moved away from town, to seek her fortune in the movies it was said.

Ryder was in fact quite a handsome young man and

always dressed well. He grew used to young girls and old ladies exchanging smiles with him as they passed in the street or in shops or restaurants. He liked to cut a dash, as the saying goes.

As the years went by a touch of grey appeared at his temples. This did not bother him at first. After all he had heard that young women liked the distinguished older man.

But sometimes he reckoned that this was simply another bit of *plámás* put out by women to keep their men-folk happy.

Still—experience, maturity, these were things women were attracted to. Along with good looks of course, and intelligence, sophistication, and to some degree—well, a large degree—money.

Dressing well was important—his suits were always tailored, with slightly hatched pockets and deeply cut vents; and of course ties were carefully chosen.

The ability to dance was a must in his younger days and he not only enjoyed dancing but danced well; that double backward step in the 'quickstep' was a specialty of his, but he could also jive to 'Blue Suede Shoes' as well as, if nor better than, most other people.

But of course real dancing disappeared with the arrival of discos. He went a few times, jollied along by some of the junior salesmen. After spending most of the evening in the pub it wasn't too bad. Then one hectic night he met two young female clerks from his local bank whom he used to deal with on a daily basis. When he asked them to dance they both shrieked with laughter and ran away. He finished his drink and got a taxi home, utterly depressed and darkly picturing himself 'cutting a dash' in an old people's home.

Ryder sighed as he looked in the mirror in his private office bathroom. With a quick movement of his hand he brushed back the thin greying hair at his temples. He turned and walked out through his office, through the reception area and out to his private parking space.

The BMW looked good parked there, it's discreet chrome glinting in the summer sun. Well, why wouldn't it look good, it had cost a fortune. He pressed his key, and with an important sounding blip! the car electronically sprang to attention, its doors unlocking and its hazard lights flashing a salute.

Ryder opened the door, and taking off his pin-striped jacket he placed it on the hanger by the back seat. A scent of warm leather oozed from the car.

He slipped into the driver's seat, started the engine, and drove slowly towards the gates of the factory, sternly resisting the temptation to smile at the glances, some admiring, some disapproving, of employees moving out into the street.

The engine was almost silent and he found himself looking at the rev counter to confirm that it was running.

The air-conditioning cut in with a soft hiss.

On the street he accelerated, moving into third and then fourth gear, a dull roar just discernable through the thick pile of the fitted carpets.

He turned left, joining the stream of cars heading for the suburbs. As he did so, he noticed a young woman walking on the footpath. She was tall, in her late twenties or so, and dressed in a dark blue suit.

He passed by and then slowed to a stop at the traffic lights. The young woman passed him, walking briskly on high heels, a large battered briefcase in one hand and a rolled newspaper in the other. The blue skirt was tight, and met a slim, lightly tanned pair of legs about three inches above the knee. The rest of the skirt encased a firm, rounded bottom that moved voluptuously but unostentatiously from side to side.

Ryder purred appreciatively.

The lights changed to green and the traffic slowly started to move again, creating a fresh cloud of pollution as accelerators and clutch pedals were alternately pressed and depressed by impatient feet. He swept past the girl, half wondering had she noticed him, and had just begun to pick up speed when the traffic slowed again for the next light.

The van in front of him was overdue a visit to the garage. He hurriedly jabbed the close button for the air intake as black fumes poured from underneath the van and slowly billowed up over the bonnet of his car, adding to the thin film of grease already accumulating there.

The girl strode by again. She had long, rich, auburn hair. Apart from dark red lipstick she did not appear to wear much make-up. She wore simple gold earrings and carried her head high with a slightly snooty expression.

"Perhaps she's had a hard day at the office," he thought.

He began to wonder what she did for a living. A solicitor possibly, or an assistant bank manager. She dropped her newspaper and bent to pick it up, immediately attracting the attention of all the male drivers, two Telecom workers and a man operating a pneumatic drill in the middle of the road. Their eyes all zeroed in on the VPL.

Ryder wondered if he should offer her a lift.

A roar of engines signaled another move forward. The van lurched in a cloud of fumes through a zebra crossing, earning a string of protests from an old lady who then turned to Ryder and raised her umbrella in a threatening manner. He stopped, smiled, and nodded to her as she gathered her dignity and tottered across the street. The girl in blue followed her and he nodded and smiled to her too. She gave him a brief glance (as one might give to something which had crawled out from under a piece of rotting wood) and marched across the street, her rolled newspaper tucked under her arm like a sergeant-major's cane, her nose in the air.

He shrugged mentally and eased the car into gear as the traffic slowly picked up speed again. A courier on a cross-country motorbike, sweating in his leathers, weaved in and out of the creeping cars, earning the silent resentment of the car drivers.

Ryder saw the girl disappear from his mirror. She was just like Catherine, he thought, even down to the lace blouse and the dark blue suit.

God! He'd never forget that first date.

They had driven into the country, found a small pub and eventually become caught up in someone's wedding celebrations.

The small pub had a small dance-floor—and a small band—and they had turned the phrase "dancing the night away" into reality. What was that tune? It still gave him that strange soppy, soft, sad feeling whenever he heard it.

They had entered the spirit of the wedding celebration, but in fact they were oblivious to everyone but each other. She had just graduated, he was on a rising curve in the business...

The stream of cars had begun to pick up speed. The turn-off to the motorway appeared and he began to negotiate his way into it. A horn blared and a sports car passed by, the driver glaring at him while silently tapping the side of his forehead. Ryder offered him a finger in return.

He pressed the accelerator and shot onto the motorway, crossing the lanes to the fast one, where he sat on the back bumper of a Citroen CV2 being driven flat out by a young man in his early twenties. Ryder resisted the urge to turn on his headlights and after some thirty seconds of glancing in his mirror the young man eased into the middle lane.

Catherine was a fast driver too, and loved to drive them to little out-of-the-way places where they could sip wine and gaze into each other's eyes. They didn't seem to need sleep. They absorbed energy from each other's eyes, fingers, lips, and later, other parts.

They dropped all their friends. They just didn't see the point of meeting anyone else when all they wanted was each other. On the rare occasions when they did join the gang she was the centre of attention. No subject was taboo and any generalisations casually dropped she eagerly pounced upon and analysed. She could swap jokes with the best. She was at ease with ambassadors as she was with actors, students or bar flies...

His speed gradually slowed down. Someone flashed lights at him and he automatically moved over to the middle lane, his hands responding to some auto-pilot as his mind flicked through his memories. He glanced almost unseeingly to his right, not really registering the passing school bus with the numerous contorted faces being made in his direction. His mind was a few thousand miles away, at a ball. Great blazing chandeliers hung high over the gleaming dance-floor. An orchestra was playing the theme from Doctor Zhivago, and he and Catherine were the most handsome couple in the great moving mass of dancers.

Distinguished gentlemen with medals and ribbons floated by, partnered by aristocratic ladies wearing tiaras. But he and Catherine did not need medals or tiaras. After the ball they had gone to an all-night wine bar and laughed and smoked and drank wine till dawn.

On an impulse he turned off at the next exit and wound his way through some narrow streets until he found a florist.

"Special occasion, is it?" the assistant asked.

"Sort of" he muttered, and searched through the flowers on offer until he found what he wanted. A dozen pink carnations.

He returned to the car and made his way back to the motorway, smiling to himself. He switched on the radio and the car was filled with the music of Louis Armstrong and "Mack the Knife." An instant picture came to mind; Catherine, jiving with a friend of his, her scarlet skirt flying in the air, her long legs whirling to the beat.

He was so deep in thought that he almost missed his exit and made a rapid and highly illegal swerve into the inside lane, very much to the annoyance of a commercial traveller whose stock-in-trade—a rack of the latest line in part dresses—piled into the front seats as he applied emergency braking. Ryder did not see him as another sharp swerve brought him onto the exit road that wound its way into a stockbroker belt of expensive houses lying snugly under large leafy trees, and partially hidden behind stone walls and high gates.

Eventually, he came to an entrance which was flanked on each side by huge chestnut trees. Their dark, leaf-clad branches, sprinkled with creamy flowers, met and mingled over the drive.

He turned in and drove slowly towards the house. The

drive was bordered on each side by a wide expanse of grass dotted by mature trees. The grass had not been cut for some time and from one of the trees an old swing hung, anchored to the undergrowth by tendrils of binderweed, its ropes green with moss. Under another tree a wooden sailing boat lurched at an angle, a flat tyre on one side of its trailer, a nest of wasps thriving in its small cabin.

The drive led to a gravelled parking area in front of a substantial two-storied house.

A tall, middle-aged woman immediately appeared at the open door. She had long grey hair down to her shoulders and wore a billowy blue dress. She was breathing heavily and her face was dark with anger.

"You're late" she shouted, "We're due at Kent's at seven o'clock."

She turned and walked impatiently back into the house.

Ryder sighed and slumped in his car seat.

"Right-oh Catherine" he muttered.

He glanced in the mirror and brushed back his thinning grey hair with his hand. He picked up the carnations, noting that they were already limp from the heat of the day.

He sighed again and moved his body—remarkably unchanged he thought, after thirty-five years of marriage— from the car.

A SHOOTING WEEKEND

Not far from Cashel, the car arrived at a pair of crumbling gateposts from which the gates had long since been removed. Beyond the gateway a potholed drive meandered through a park, protected from curious cattle by a buckled and paint-hungry cast-iron fence. The cattle were easily distracted, there being little else in the park but themselves and a selection of giant thistles and docks, both species long past their seed-casting days.

Soon the car reached a wide sweep of gravel on which a Georgian house of some character stood. Apart from one feature of its architecture it was a standard Georgian country house of the late 18th century. The one exception in its design was that a tower or turret had been built into one of the four corners of the building at the whim of its first owner. The elegant yet practical building had seen many owners in its life, including an unpopular landlord who, in fear of his tenants, had taken the precaution of installing steel shutters on all the windows and a quarter-inch steel plate behind the front door. Even the beautiful fanlight over this door was guarded from the inside by a fan-shaped series of iron spikes. Alas, all these precautions came to naught when an assassin gained access to the roof and thence to a skylight from where he shot the landlord as he reposed on the lavatory.

Various owners followed, minor gentry and successful businessmen, all of whom loved the place and the salmon to be found in plenty in the swift, deep River Suir which flowed through the gently sloping fields beneath the house. But wars and economic depression were to have their way, and for decades the house lay empty, its old steel shutters and utter isolation protecting it from vandals.

Then, along came John Redpath, a Scotsman, an eccentric, and a man with a mission—he would restore Meadow House to its former glory.

Redpath's plan was simple. To pay for the restoration of the house he would follow the example of others elsewhere and run the old place as a country guesthouse. People would come for the fishing and shooting and would be treated as invited guests, or even as old friends. After a day in the countryside, engaged in outdoor pursuits, they would enjoy dinner with his family, and relax with brandies around the drawing room fire.

Only when guests were leaving after their stay would money be mentioned—in a discreet, casual undertone of course.

This formula worked reasonably well, and although there was never enough money for major work, there was enough to repair the roof and fill the house with a whimsical collection of old, second-hand furniture which gave the place an air of long-established shabby gentility entirely in keeping with John Redpath and his family.

It was to this house that McFadden came, one October day, at the urging of his friend Kennedy, to spend a weekend shooting snipe.

Kennedy was a successful architect who had inherited a partnership in one of the leading architectural practices in the city. His relationship with McFadden came somewhere between acquaintanceship and close friendship.

Kennedy's precise ways—his life carefully planned out so that the done thing was always done; his constant awareness of his position in local society—were a source of both amusement and fascination for McFadden whose somewhat erratic career as an estate agent with marital problems was in sharp contrast to Kennedy's regimented and rock steady life.

From childhood, Kennedy's mother and father had always seen to it that every eventuality was taken care of. When he started school his mother gave him a bag of sweets with the instruction,

"Make sure you give some to the biggest boy in the class."

A couple of years later he was given an expensive cricket set to bring to school with him so that he would always be on the team.

When he was ten, his father went to London and bought him an English-made, double-barreled shotgun, when English guns were still reasonably priced, which was carefully stored and then presented to him on his twenty-first birthday.

As a young man Kennedy carried on this tradition of organisation and exactness. Wine was laid down years in advance of every occasion, just as offspring were entered for boarding school within hours of their birth. Books were subscribed to, new art galleries were patronised, and the right people were entertained.

McFadden's parents, on the other hand, though kindly and loving, were less well-off, rather reserved, and somewhat suspicious of anything that smacked of social climbing. It was with some apprehension therefore, that they had sent young McFadden to board at a well-known public school, run by Catholic priests.

He hated everything about it, from the enforced confinement and lack of freedom to the colourless, mass-produced meals. As far as his parents were concerned, the school may have toughened him up a bit and given him a sense of independence, but it also gave him ideas 'above his station.'

Years later, to his eternal, cringing shame, he would remember his sullen embarrassment when his parents came to visit him in a Ford Prefect while the parents of his school pals came up the drive in Jaguars and Mercedes-Benzs.

When home on holidays the young McFadden spent much of his time hanging around the centre of his provincial home town, in or outside the one or two coffee houses the place had to offer. His teenage pals came from all walks of life, and some of them would have been disapproved of by both the Kennedy and McFadden parents.

After school and an unsuccessful year at college, McFadden emigrated to London and embarked on a career in property management which was to take him around the world. Returning twelve years later, with five children and an American wife, he opened an estate agency business in the town.

In contrast to that of McFadden, Kennedy's early career went on straight and steady lines. He attended the same primary and early secondary school as McFadden, and then went off to an even more prestigious public school run by monks, before studying architecture and ending up with a master's degree from Oxford. Then it was back to the family firm, a suitable wife, and a future in which every facet of his life, with the possible exception of death, would be totally organised.

Nevertheless, the two men were relaxed in each other's company and shared a sense of humour and a fondness for old country houses, shooting, and wine….

As the car pulled up at the front door, John Redpath appeared on the steps. He had a friendly, confident face, a full red beard, and an Oxford drawl. He wore a chequered lumberjack's shirt and a tight pair of moleskin trousers held up with braces. He and Kennedy greeted each other like old school pals, which in fact they were, and when McFadden had been introduced they were brought into the hall. Several gangly children then appeared and took care of their luggage, while the proprietor led them into the drawing room.

This was a very comfortable place, nicely scented with the perfume of many log fires, and furnished with deep, comfortable and well-used sofas and armchairs.

Faded rugs lay here and there on the polished, wooden floor, and a coffee table was hidden under a large collection of *Country Life* magazines, some of considerable antiquity. On the walls were dark portraits of gloomy-looking men and women wearing eighteenth and nineteenth century clothes. Visitors often remarked at the family likeness to the Redpath family though the paintings had in fact been bought at knock-down prices at various country house auctions.

After offering them tea, served in a pretty Mason's Ironstone set, and catching up on their latest news, Redpath showed them to their room.

All the rooms in Meadow House were large and most contained two beds and when Redpath offered the Turret

Room they immediately agreed to share it. Kennedy picked one bed at random and immediately began to unpack his bag with great care, placing various items of toiletry on the wash-hand-basin and carefully hanging each item of clothing in the wardrobe. Two pairs of shoes, one a pair of highly polished brogues and the other a pair of suede boots (brothel creepers McFadden called them) were laid carefully at the end of his bed.

McFadden threw his bag in a corner and then explored the curious turret at the corner of the room. The small circular room with a conical ceiling had been converted to a bathroom with a large cast-iron bath, a wash-hand basin and a toilet, all in olive green. He placed his tooth brush on the wash-hand basin and returned to the bedroom where Kennedy was cleaning his suede shoes with a special rubber brush and whistling tunelessly.

McFadden lay down on his bed with his arms behind his head. He glanced at his own battered boots and decided that the polish he had given them last week was still good for a day or two.

When Kennedy had finished unpacking they sauntered downstairs and were each handed a generous glass of sherry which they sipped standing in front of a roaring fire in the drawing room before being shown to their seats at the dining room table. There were no other guests so they were joined by Redpath and his wife Sarah.

The dinner was excellent—a seafood vol-au-vent followed by a choice of wild poached salmon or roast pork. McFadden was the only one to opt for the pork and had two helpings.

John Redpath was generous with his wine, no doubt it would appear somewhere on the bill, and the conversation was lively.

Redpath told of his difficulty in getting good television reception and explained in considerable detail his plan to erect an aerial attached to a "gaseous sphere" on the end of a rope. The "gaseous sphere" would be allowed to float to a great height thus ensuring a good signal. Kennedy, with a sidelong glance in McFadden's direction, advised caution.

The plans for the next day were then discussed. Kennedy and McFadden would spend most of it out on the never-ending bog, walking up snipe, and then as the day drew to a close, might have a go at the evening flight of duck over the swollen river which flowed silently past the meadow at the front of the house.

Redpath was quite interested in their shooting plans.

"I've bought a gun you know" he said, producing for their approval a long, single-barrelled shotgun of Russian manufacture.

"I haven't had a chance for a shot yet but perhaps I might join you for the evening flight?"

"Yes of course" muttered Kennedy, throwing another sidelong glance at McFadden, and ever so slightly rolling his eyes,

"We'd be delighted."

After coffee and a liqueur the two paying guests asked to be excused and went up to their bedroom.

Kennedy, with lots of grunts and splashing of water, fastidiously washed his teeth and got ready for bed while McFadden rummaged in his weekend bag, eventually finding a flattened tube of toothpaste. As he brushed his teeth his stomach made a loud and ominous gurgling sound—he just had time to slam the door shut, drop his trousers and throw himself on the toilet.

But there was to be no quick relief. He was obliged to remain in the turret for over an hour as the loud noises of his misfortune echoed up and around him (the next day he would hear that Redpath had appeared at the bedroom door in his pyjamas and asked Kennedy if any assistance was required).

Eventually, he was able to return to the bedroom. Kennedy had obviously been asleep for some time and now lay mouth agape, snoring loudly.

McFadden sighed and got into bed.

When the old-fashioned alarm clock on the table between the two beds went off like a firm alarm McFadden groaned.

Kennedy grinned at him.

"Weren't you the noisy one last night ? Well, you had better get a move on. We can't keep the gillie waiting you know."

Although at first a bit queasy, McFadden did feel better after a large fried breakfast, and by the time they had loaded their gear into the car a healthy sweat was removing the remains of whatever evil he had swallowed with the pork. Nevertheless he vowed never to eat a member of that particular species again.

A short drive brought them to the edge of the bog where they met Paddy, who was to be their guide or gillie for the day. He was a small, quiet-spoken man of a serious disposition who welcomed them with the tip of his finger to his cap. He gravely pointed out that as a member of the local gun club he would have to restrict them, as agreed, to shooting only snipe and nothing else.

"Absolutely, of course" they assured him, and, hitching up their game bags they followed him out onto the bog.

The next few hours proved to be disappointing. Either the snipe were on holiday, or some devastating disease had overcome them.

Walking up a bog in a line wearing heavy waders, carrying a full belt of cartridges, gun held forward, eyes flicking intently from left to right, sweat trickling down your back under your waterproof Barbour, can be a very tiring business after three or four hours.

Even Paddy, whose face could normally be described as expressionless, was beginning to look exasperated.

At noon they paused for sandwiches and tea from a flask, and then examined their game bags.

Kennedy had shot four snipe, McFadden two. The guide, even though he carried a gun, had not fired a shot.

They munched their sandwiches in silence. McFadden opened his game bag and took out a bottle of Power's Gold Label whiskey.

"Here, come on now, this will cheer you up."

He insisted on pouring a good measure into their mugs, and within a short time spirits had risen considerably. The conversation picked up, their meal was finished with some gusto and, before they could refuse, McFadden had given them the remainder of the whiskey.

By the time they had put away their mugs and sandwich boxes even Paddy was cracking jokes and talking to his charges as if he had known them for years, and it was with a light heart that they carried on across the bog and into the afternoon.

However, after an hour Kennedy and McFadden had shot only one more snipe each. Considering that one snipe contains less than three ounces of meat this was not good. Where are the great flocks of snipe they had been told about they wondered.

They came to a ditch which divided one man's bog from another. Suddenly, there was a great clatter of wings and a large, gleaming, mature cock pheasant rose in front of them. Each of the three reacted, all within less than two seconds.

Without thinking and without hesitation, Kennedy

fired first, one barrel after the other, and missed, although a feather flew off the bird (rather like part of a bomber being blown off by anti-aircraft fire McFadden reflected later).

Paddy the guide, whose gun had been silent all day, then fired, in frustration, desperation, or just high spirits, they would never know. But he missed too.

A split second later, McFadden threw up his gun from the hip, not really expecting to hit the bird, more as a reflex action than anything else. He fired one barrel, the pheasant immediately folded and dived into the ground.

They all looked at it, Kennedy and Paddy quite willing to believe that it was their shot which actually killed the bird.

"My bird I think, chaps," said McFadden, picking it up with a sigh of satisfaction and stuffing it, with some difficulty, into his game bag.

Kennedy and Paddy looked at each other, shrugged and walked on, ignoring McFadden's "Wait for me lads"

The shooting party arrived back at Meadow House just as the sun was beginning to set. Kennedy paid off their guide and then he and McFadden had a cup of tea in their room before preparing themselves for a go at the evening flight of duck on the river below the house.

Light No. 8 cartridges used for the snipe were removed from their cartridge belts and replaced with No. 5s.

Kennedy then took something made of dark polished wood out of his bag and showed it to McFadden.

"This should help matters" he said; "It's a duck lure; I had it sent over from Canada."

He blew into the mouthpiece and produced a definite 'quack'. McFadden was impressed.

In the back hall they pulled on their waders and made their way down towards the river.

It soon became evident that the river was in spate and a great expanse of the meadow was flooded. Here and there wild shrubs and trees stood like little desert islands in a calm sea.

McFadden decided to take up a position leaning against a small ash tree while Kennedy waded further into the flood and concealed himself in a willow bush.

Time passed, the pink streaks on the horizon faded away, and the night grew darker.

There was no sighting of any duck, and the only sound to be heard was the squeaky "Quack, quack" from Kennedy's bush.

Soon it was almost pitch black. The "Quack, quack" ceased, and Kennedy, looking cross and out of breath, splashed his way back to McFadden.

"Come on, lets go, it's a waste of time here."

Just then there was a great swish of wings. They quickly raised their guns and just as quickly lowered them again as a flock of swans flew majestically over their heads, heading for their night quarters.

Kennedy sighed, switched on a torch, and the two of them made their way back to the house.

They were met in the hall by a jovial Redpath, and when they had changed out of their waders he invited them into the drawing room for a drink. He gave each of them a Waterford crystal goblet, and then busied himself opening a bottle of wine.

"I must celebrate" he said, smiling, "I followed you lads down to the meadow with my new gun."

"Did you really?" said Kennedy, one hand in the pocket of his corduroy trousers and the other holding his crystal goblet expectantly.

"Yes" said Redpath—puffing a bit as he tried to extract the cork— "and do you know, there was this damn duck sitting in a bush; it wouldn't come out but kept quacking away. I was very tempted to fire straight into the bush y'know, but I though it would be regarded as unsporting."

The loud "Pop" of the cork was followed instantly by the crash of broken glass on the wooden floor.

McFadden and Redpath looked around.

Kennedy stood by the fireplace, his empty hand still holding an imaginary goblet, the blood draining from his normally rosy cheeks.

"Would you mind if I just had a large brandy?" he said.

GALE FORCE

Despite the warm June sun, a chilly breeze blew through the graveyard on the hill.

Pat Moore stood on the fringe of the huge crowd gathered around the grave. It was impossible to get any closer, even if he had wanted to. The priest's words drifted to him on the wind,

"…..may the perpetual light shine upon him, may he rest in peace…."

The crowd responded in unison with a deep "Amen".

On the wind a faint but audible chattering came from the vicinity of three red-faced old men near the gate. One or two mourners turned with looks of annoyance but the gaze of hundreds of heads, bowed in grief or respect, remained focused on the gleaming oak coffin resting on two beams over the grave.

"Well, there's an end to it" thought Moore to himself.

He looked out over the graveyard wall and down across green fields and hedges to where the sea glimmered peacefully right out to the horizon, and thought of a night just four months previously, almost to the day.....

The wind had started to freshen early in the week. Each day it moved a little further up the Beaufort Scale.

By Tuesday evening it had moved from 'A Moderate Breeze', number Four on the scale, to 'Strong Breeze', number Six on the scale.

By Wednesday it had moved through number Seven to Force Eight, or Gale Force. There it stayed through Wednesday and most of Thursday, lulling the fishermen into a false sense of security. Yes, it was rough, but nothing they had not dealt with before.

This wind came from the South West, sweeping in over a thousand miles or more of the Atlantic Ocean before being combed by the rugged coastline of Southern Ireland. It pushed the sea before it, firstly in grey-green swells that crashed onto the shore from Mizen Head to Hook Head. Then, as its power increased, it whipped the tops off the swells so that waves began to break far out at sea.

When it behaves itself and stays between Force 4 and Force 6, this wind is known to fishermen as a 'whiting wind', a wind which brings welcome shoals of whiting onto the fishing grounds. But this was February, the beginning of a short season when cod, in their hundreds of thousands, come in close to shore to spawn. And this time the wind did bring cod, lots of cod. The shoals were less than ten miles off, so the trawlers did not have to make a two or three day trip, but could return at the end of the day laden with the glistening green, valuable fish.

On Thursday the boats had put to sea in the early hours of that morning knowing it was going to be rough but also knowing that a gale could break up the shoals causing the cod to disperse and move away.

The wind freshened in the morning, and on the national radio service the Sea Area Weather Forecast was giving "Gales or Strong Gales, Force Eight or Nine". The BBC (always referred to as "the Englishman") gave a similar forecast.

Now the various crews of the small fleet gritted their teeth. The men on deck, in between the time the net was shot and hauled, a period of less than three hours in this good fishing, gutted and washed the catch, while glancing one moment at the sweeping, risen sea around them and then surreptitiously at the skipper in the wheelhouse, willing him to call it a day.

In the individual boats, each skipper stared out through the rain and spray-streaked wheelhouse window, both hands firmly on the wheel, turning slightly off course from time to time to dodge a particularly bad wave, then returning on course and glancing back through the aft window at the bar-taut wire cables towing the net.

Up to this point a dangerous sense of complacency had prevailed in the fleet. In previous years boats would not normally go to sea if the weatherman gave winds of Force Seven to Eight. But the days of big fishing had gone, and now every day had to be worked if at all possible. Besides, recent gale forecasts had never quite materialised and the strength of these winds had crept up slowly during the week, perhaps bringing a false sense of confidence to the fishermen.

Meanwhile the catches were mighty and the skippers and most of the crew were happy to keep hauling and re-shooting the gear.

In between hauling in the nets and stowing away the fish, and while the boats were towing, the crew wedged themselves in corners of the galley and devoted one half of their minds to a game of cards over spilled tea while performing intricate feats of mental arithmetic to calculate, to the nearest Euro, their total share of the week's catch.

Some might prefer to re-read a dog-eared magazine, while trying to ignore the increasing roll and crash of the hull as the skipper dodged from one mountain of water to another.

Earlier in the evening there had been banter on the VHF radio, with skippers trying to guess what catch their rivals had.

As the wind increased and moved towards Gale Force Nine, or Strong Gale, one skipper suggested casually over the air-waves that it might be time to turn for home.

And here a devilish stupidity intervened for a crucial

half hour or so as another skipper answered,

"You go ahead cap'n, we'll stay on awhile, we're quite comfortable here".

The use of the word 'captain' could be taken as a jeer, a wise-crack. Something was being implied. None of the boats turned but continued to plow onwards into the wind, their hawsers at breaking point.

Ashore, ten or eleven miles away, white water was crashing over the pier of the little fishing village while rain drummed on the roof of the fish auction hall. The auction floor was empty, the smaller half-deckers having remained tied up in port that day. The foreman, Toddy, played a water hose on the already spotless, smooth concrete floor.

From his house on a promontory overlooking the harbour, Moore, the Co-op manager, sat in a swivel chair looking out the big window at the sheets of rain sweeping across the harbour in the light of the arc lamps positioned at intervals along the pier. Behind him his VHF radio hummed and whistled.

From time to time the room would be filled with the voice of a skipper contacting another boat, exchanging information in quick, business-like comments as the trawlers crashed through another towering wave. Every second word was a swear word, and yet these snatches of conversation were matter-of-fact, almost laconic, although the manager could detect the tension in their voices.

Then there was a change. One skipper, (Moore was pretty sure it was Paddy Haughton, the unofficial leader of the small fleet) asked another to call him on his private channel. These so-called private channels were set up by their radio dealers but were not always private. Many trawlers had sophisticated scanning devices which could track down most 'private' channels.

Moore continued to listen to the unbroken hiss of the static. No one else came on to speak for some time which meant that most of the other boats were probably scanning all the channels to find out what the two skippers had to talk about.

He jumped when the phone rang. It was Breda Haughton. The radio she had in her kitchen was a lot more sophisticated than the one he had.

She was brief and to the point,

"Paddy's been on. Someone's been lost overboard."

"Is it one of Paddy's lads?" asked Moore.

"No, it's that new boat, you know, Sullivan—Paddy asked me to tell you."

She hung up without saying anything else. She probably had other calls to make.

Moore walked to the window and looked out towards the sea. It was pitch black, all he could see was sheets of spray flying under the swaying harbour lights.

It was almost an hour before trawler lights appeared, swinging up and down on the huge swell outside the harbour wall.

Night or day, whether the observer be a landlubber or an old sea dog, a trawler coming home on a stormy sea always held the eye. In really bad weather the crew would have gathered behind the skipper in the wheel house. There would be no one working out on the deck, where white water would occasionally break over the winch, the clamped down hatch, and the pounds filled with ungutted fish.

Two boats came rolling around the breakwater and into the relatively calm harbour waters. They moved slowly up to the discharging berth outside the auction hall. Ropes were thrown and caught by willing hands on shore.

Glancing out into the darkness Moore saw other lights approaching the harbour. He pulled on a hooded waterproof jacket and went down to the auction hall berth, heading straight for Sullivan's boat.

He was surprised to find that the crew, though silent and pale-faced, were working away gutting and washing the catch. It has to be done, he thought to himself. He asked after the skipper but was told that he was on the phone talking to the police and emergency services. He could not bring himself to ask who had been lost but the mate, seeing his predicament, took him aside and told him.

"It's young Eamonn, Eamonn Kelly."

"What age is— was he?" Moore asked.

"Nineteen, this day last week" said the mate, clearing his throat and spitting into the harbour before climbing back on board the trawler.

After waiting for a while Moore was about to return to his office when Sullivan came out of the wheelhouse and jumped onto the pier.

"Can I use your office phone—there's calls I have to make and I'd prefer a land line."

He looked gaunt, his face pale under a three day stubble.

"He was gone over in a second you know—caught up in the gear. We did everything we could, stopped engines, then hauled in the gear—nearly got knocked over by a fucking monster of a wave. He wasn't in the net anyway. We called the helicopter and searched for four, maybe five hours—Jesus I put the rest of the crew at risk, turning in that sea. He's fucking gone and that's all there is to it."

Moore let him into the office and stayed outside in the corridor. But through the opaque glass of the door he saw him hunched over the phone, heard him breaking the awful news to some family on the west coast. He saw his blurred outline double over, heard his deep sobs.

Moore turned away. He went down to the harbour and watched the fish from Sullivan's boat being laid out for the auction…...

A decade of the rosary was being said now. The priest

calling out the Hail Mary in a strong voice—the congregation replying in a low mumble from which an individual late voice could occasionally be heard;

"…..now and at the hour of our death. Amen"

Most of the fishing community were there. Big men, with red faces and red hands and black and silver hair shiny with oil, on one knee in the grass. Younger men with shaven heads and tattoos leaned awkwardly against the stone wall of the graveyard. Women of all ages, the older ones probably thinking of others they had accompanied to this lonely field, the younger ones crying quietly, wiping tears from their eyes with sodden, rolled up tissues, thinking of a birthday party in the pub last week.….

As soon as the storm had moderated to some degree, every man with a sound boat, big or small, had put to sea to find Eamonn Kelly. They rode the swell that still remained after the gale, combing the waters of the fishing grounds and dodging in and out of the bays and coves.

All along the shore, men, women and children of all ages searched for what in their hearts they dreaded to find.

Baskets of fishermen's boots, gloves and other items of clothing were collected from miles of coastline in the slim hope that they might be something belonging to Eamonn Kelly.

One morning, a few days after the tragedy, when in spite of all the searching there had been no sign of a body, Eamonn's family appeared at the door of Moore's office. The group consisted of the father and mother, a younger son and two sisters. Their eyes were red from grief and tiredness. He invited them in, brought in odd chairs from other rooms and offered them tea.

They needed his help they said. There was this man in Tipperary who was a psychic. He would tell them where to find poor Eamonn, but the whole thing had to be co-ordinated they explained.

Moore nodded sympathetically while wondering what they had in mind.

The father, a strong-looking man with a weather-beaten face, squirmed awkwardly in his chair as he tried to explain to Moore.

"You see, Matty Sullivan and the lads are out at sea with a herring net looking for Eamonn. The're searchin' the area where he was lost. But the thing is, Mr. O'Neill in Tipperary will be able to guide them if you would be the go-between, you know, by using the VHF and the phone".

Moore nodded several times. It was of course unusual, but he was ready to do anything which might be of the smallest use.

He immediately phoned the number which Eamonn's father gave to him and spoke to Mr. O'Neill.

"Do you have the sea chart for the area?" inquired

O'Neill in a straightforward, businesslike manner.

"Yes, its in front of me now." said Moore.

"Well, do you see a headland called Ram's Head? That's the place to search. Tell your friend in the boat."

Moore said;

"Can you tell me how close they should go?"

O'Neill thought for a moment.

"Tell him to go in to about two miles off the headland and search along there" he said.

Moore then called up Matty Sullivan's trawler on the VHF.

"*Sea Quest, Sea Quest*, do you receive me, over ?"

Matty had been expecting his call and was quick to respond.

"Gettin' you loud and clear, loud and clear."

He sighed, and then continued; "You've spoken to this gentleman I understand, have you? Well, we're standing by, what do you want us to do, over ?"

Moore cleared his throat and glanced awkwardly towards the Kelly family before passing on the instructions to Sullivan.

The *Sea Quest* acknowledged and then went off the air. Biscuits and fruit cake were found for the Kelly family, and more tea was brewed.

Moore found it difficult to keep a conversation going as an hour, then two hours, then three went by.

The family was deep in grief, and finding Eamonn's body would not cure that but would let them bring the terrible business to an end.

At mid-day Matty called back and asked for new instructions. Mr. O'Neill was contacted and spent some time deliberating over his chart in Tipperary before designating a new search area. Eamonn's body was now off another headland he said. Moore passed this on to Matty who asked him to enquire at what depth Eamonn's body was floating.

There was a long pause as O'Neill deliberated once more.

"He'll be floating eight to ten feet below the surface" he said.

And so it went on.

The family left in mid afternoon but were shyly gathered at the door at 8.30 next morning.

After four days Matty phoned Moore in the night time.

"This can't go on, I'm sorry. The crew want to help but they're stretched to breaking point and so am I. This is like lookin' for a needle in a fuckin' haystack."

There was the tinkling noise of a pub in the background.

"I understand, Matty," Moore told him. "Thanks for all your help. I'll explain to the family."

Moore broke the news to the Kellys when they arrived early the next morning. They did not seem to be surprised. They thanked him and asked him to thank Mr. O'Neill and Matty and immediately shuffled out of his office. They too were exhausted and were going home…..

Moore felt the warm sun on his back as he watched the crowds slowly stream out of the graveyard. The people were talking now; he heard yet another muffled burst of laughter, something which always amazed him at funerals.

There had been no sign of Eamon's body for months. After a couple of weeks of searching nearly everyone had given up the task. Traditionally, and as a matter of grim fact, it was thought that most bodies lost at sea would rise to the surface for a time as the gases in the corpse expanded. There was some argument as to the number of days it took for this to happen. Water temperatures, food consumed, clothes worn and other factors played a part, but it was generally agreed that after seven to nine days the corpse floated to the surface for a brief period, and if it was not quickly recovered it would disappear forever.

Moore was surprised then to hear from Breda Haughton after nearly four months.

"Eamonn's body has been found. He's going to the chapel tonight, burial tomorrow morning."

As usual she was brief and to the point and had rushed away to make other phone calls.

There was a huge crowd at the chapel that night, the family downcast and silent, and friends and shipmates cowed by the occasion and a sort of relief that at last Eamonn had been found and could now be laid to rest

But there were plenty of tears shed at the funeral mass next morning. Eamonn's hurley and his club jersey were laid on the fine carved oak coffin. Young brother, sisters and cousins made the customary little contributions to the service, grasping the podium with knuckles as white as their drawn faces.

The priest's sermon was soft, considerate, thoughtful, and when he spoke of the place in heaven for Eamonn, it was with complete conviction, and Moore, fighting with his agnosticism, could almost believe it to be true....

By now, the graveyard was almost empty. The fine coffin had been lowered with ease into the ground by the two local grave diggers, who then covered the grave with green beige, on top of which were placed numerous wreaths.

As Moore stood there, Breda Haughton walked slowly up to him.

"They must have laid out a small fortune for that coffin" said Moore, always interested in the financial side of things.

"True, considering there's almost nothing in it" said Breda, quietly.

When Moore raised his eyebrows she told him the story.

Four months, give or take a day, since the night of the gale, a trawler from up the coast had hauled its net. Out on the deck spilled a disappointing catch of small spotted dogfish, pouting, and weed. As the crew began to sweep it over the side they saw what appeared to be part of a human skull in the middle of it. The skipper, who hated red tape and the forms that had to be filled out on occasions like this, was about to shovel it over the side when he was restrained by the mate. The jawbone was pushed into a plastic bag and, when the boat arrived back in port, was handed over to the local police, with precise details of where and when it was found. They quickly put two and two together, and, in a very short time, through dental records, it was identified as the mortal remains of Eamonn Kelly.

Breda stopped talking and looked back towards the grave where the Kelly family still stood, holding on to each other for comfort. The gravediggers had removed the green cloth and the flowers and had begun to shovel earth onto the coffin.

A large coffin, thought Moore, with just part of a skull in it.

Breda spoke softly,

"Some people think it's odd, but really it's perfectly natural. That grave is where Eamonn is, his name will be on the stone and they can come here to talk to him or just to remember him. I suppose in a practical sense it's a kind of closure as they say nowadays."

She walked slowly towards the graveyard gate.

Moore nodded to himself and then followed her.

As he passed out through the gate he glanced down towards the harbour where the masts of the fishing fleet waved gently back and forwards in the light swell, and then swung his gaze westwards over the glistening blue, tranquil sea.

They'll all be heading for the fishing grounds to-night, he thought to himself, closing the gate behind him.

MOLLY

It was a typical Irish spring, Ryan thought as he drove
the Land Rover up the lane to the house, the large
wheels of the vehicle throwing water and mud onto the
ditches on either side, where the primroses struggled to
push out their flowers. Having reached the house, he
wiped his shoes on the mat and unlocked the front door.
Once inside he opened the large wooden postbox . In it
was the usual batch of bills and junk mail, but also a
roughly parceled, brown paper package addressed to
him in an uneven hand. He put the rest of the post aside
to be dealt with later and opened the parcel. It contained
a leather-bound copy of *The Imitation of Christ*,
published in Dublin in 1881, by M.H. Gill & Son. Inside
the cover was a jagged piece of lined copy-book paper
with a message scrawled on it in pencil,

"To be passed on to Pat Ryan who is related to the
O'Briens."

He opened the leather covers. In the flyleaf was the
inscription, "Walter O'Brien, Ballylough, Co.
Waterford, got this book December 31st 1881."

Ryan turned the old prayer-book over in his hand.

He was surprised, pleased and saddened at the same time. He knew the old O'Brien house had finally been sold. He did not know to whom, the whole area having been infiltrated with prosperous strangers riding on the wave of the Celtic tiger. He was pleased that he had been associated with the O'Brien family, but saddened and perhaps guilty that the association was little deserved, as, since his return from Canada a few years ago, he had been completely preoccupied with his own affairs to the extent that he had neglected the once treasured association with the fading remnants of that family.

He took off his coat, went into the living room and fell into an armchair, caressing the shiny, thick leather covers of the book. His surroundings vanished as he remembered a warm summer night in Montreal, just a few years ago....

It was in the early hours of the morning; he was standing in the living room of his apartment on Lincoln Avenue, staring out the window. It was an old style apartment, with high ceilings and spacious rooms. The huge sash windows were wide open and even though it was nearly three o'clock in the morning a constant stream of traffic noise echoed from the nearby Sherbrooke Street. The apartment did not have air conditioning so there was no point in closing the window. He glanced at the thermometer on the old-fashioned mantle piece. Ninety one degrees Farenheit.

He returned to the bedroom where his wife tossed and turned, trying desperately to find the coolest posture so that she might sleep. The sounds of a party across the courtyard drifted into the room. He went to the window and looked out. Two scantily-clad girls stood on the balcony of the apartment opposite. They saw him immediately and gave him a cheeky curtsy before passing back through the curtains. For a moment he caught a glimpse of a packed, low-lit room, with couples in close embrace dancing to a slow jazzy tune. Patches of laughter and music drifted across the courtyard.

He sighed and returned to the bed, where he lay on his back, leaving the bedclothes at his feet, where they had been abandoned. He could feel the heat radiating from his wife six inches away.

His thoughts drifted away—to Ireland, and Irish summers. If the temperature managed to reach 75 degrees for a few days it would be regarded as a great heat wave. People would walk around fanning themselves, striped awnings would be brought down from the attics of large and small town houses alike to protect the paint on the front door, and assorted cotton garments of some antiquity would be carefully aired and then worn.

A wave of operatic singing drifted from another apartment across the courtyard. How far away Ireland seemed, and yet his mind envisioned a scene in the old country, the long beach at Woodstown, where the sun had warmed the sands and children shrieked with delight as the low waves laid siege to their sandcastles, and a warm easterly breeze raised little whirlwinds of sand, infiltrating the sandwiches which mothers had carefully prepared that morning, but which the children would eagerly eat and wash down with weak tea or lemonade, not bothered by the gritty texture of the meal.

His life was deeply tied to Woodstown beach, or strand as it was referred to then. He had paddled there as a child, and the old family photo album showed him eating his first (post war) banana there, as his father fished for bass at the shoreline.

He had learned to swim there, avoiding his father's offers to teach him, which would surely have ended in disaster, and starting by himself with a panicky doggie's paddle, moving on to what he thought of as a superior side stroke. He loved to dive under the water and catch glimpses of small fish darting away. Sometimes he would dive underwater to impress other children, fiercely holding his breath for as long as possible, nonchalantly surfacing a minute or so later and glancing around furtively to see if he had impressed any of the tubby little girls who splashed nearby.

Then, as the sun began to set, mothers and fathers would call an end to the day, bathing togs would be swung and wrung to extract the last drops of salt water, and the children would sit on the gritty back seat for the drive home, crushed together in the little Ford.

Halfway to town, the car would stop at a small thatched farmhouse to visit Molly, a close friend of the family ever since she and Ryan's grandmother, as young women, had sailed for America on the Cunard line, way back in the Twenties. For grandmother, who was relatively well-off, it was a trip of curiosity, to see this much vaunted New World, to spend some money on the vampish clothes of New York

For Molly, a tall strong country girl with little prospect at home in a land of depressed, poor young farmers, it was a chance to do well, perhaps meet a young man with drive and an appreciation for a strong young woman with an open mind to new ways, willing to work hard and invest herself in the future.

Grandmother had a return ticket, Molly a single fare emigrant's admittance card, but when a telegram came to their hotel informing Molly that her father was seriously ill, Grandmother lent her the money to pay for the return journey.

There followed a few but valuable years of her young life, looking after an ailing father, her mother having succumbed to tuberculosis a few years before.

The father never recovered, and Molly was left, the woman of the house, with a brother who never married, any prospective brides evaluating the small return the farm made, the prospect of another woman in the house, kindly but strong-willed, and instead took the mailboat to England.

And so the years went by.

After the outing at Woodstown, the Ryan's small Ford would swing into the farmyard, to be greeted by Molly, wiping the flour from her apron, and her brother Tom, wiping the sweat from his forehead with his cap.

For Molly, the visit was a break in her routine of butter-making, of cooking, of making bread, of washing, of feeding the chickens whose eggs were the source of her meagre pocket money. For Tom, it was a source of pleasure to see the young ones wrestle with the newborn calves, and to some degree of annoyance, to see the children climb his hay stacks in the haggard and dislodge the protective reed topping as they slid gleefully down. For the children, it was like a visit to a fun fair, followed by a treat of warm, homemade currant bread, sweetened by honey….

In Montreal Ryan awoke, feeling sticky and tired, feeling that he should see if he could stretch his overdraft and have the apartment air-conditioned.

It was his own fault really. When he first viewed the apartment, he had looked with approval at the old-fashioned pitch pine doors, the high ceilings, the maple floors and the magnificent marble fireplace. The latter was the clinching factor, although the apartment had good, solid, if a little old-fashioned, central heating. Of all things he loved a roaring log fire in winter. The Canadians did also but had moved on to high quality heating systems and low ceilings. But this was an old-fashioned, 19th century building, with large, cast iron radiators.

In the first winter of their occupancy, enjoying one of those deceptively sunny afternoons typical of Montreal in late winter, he had left a window open and gone to bed, to awake the next day and find that the deep, overnight frost had frozen the radiator, which subsequently burst asunder and flooded the apartment below much to the annoyance of the two gay men who lived there.......

The phone rang, bringing Ryan back to the present in Ireland. He answered it and received instructions from his wife concerning the casserole in the oven.

"OK darling, 200 degrees, right I've got that, I'll put it on straight away, OK, see you later."

He went into the kitchen, checked that the casserole was in fact in the oven, and switched it on at 200 degrees as instructed. He returned to his armchair...

As a small boy, he had a tendency to run away when he was not getting his own way. Once, aged six, he had taken his tricycle and ridden more than eight miles away, down the road in the direction of Cork, stopping at a railroad crossing to listen to the song of a cuckoo which perched on a tree nearby. For provisions he had brought a large orange and a tablespoon in his schoolbag. After eating the orange he pedaled on for a mile or two more but soon felt weary and began to cry. Fortunately, he was rescued by a postman, who managed to get his address from him, and, having squeezed his tricycle into the back of his van amongst a lot of canvass bags, then drove him home.

His mother tucked him, sobbing, into his bed where he slept for twelve hours. Nothing was ever said to him, his childish exhaustion being deemed sufficient punishment.

Young Ryan then found that it was easier to pretend that he was running away and to simply hide in the loft over the kitchen. There he could hear the concerned voices of his mother and the housekeeper wondering where he had got to. This would eventually get to him and his guilt would make him reappear in the house after an hour or two. In later years he often wondered if they knew where he was all along.

One summer, however, he ran away to the O'Brien's house at Ballyvoreen. He was three years older now, so he had a small, but proper, two-wheeled bicycle. He was well received by Molly and Tom, the latter bringing the youngster with him to fetch the milking cows from the field and giving him little jobs to do as the cows were milked by hand.

Molly took out her bike and cycled off, apparently to

do some messages.

Later in the afternoon he heard a car approach the farmyard and, encouraged by Tom, hid behind a water barrel which collected water from the roof of the milking parlour.

The visitor was his mother, who did not appear to be worried, but was overheard to say to Molly, who had since returned from her messages,

"Molly, young Pat has run away, if by any chance you see him, would you please give him these Wellington boots?"

Molly said she would indeed, the two women smiling at each other.

The next two weeks would remain a treasure in Pat's memory for the rest of his life, and he would often draw on them in discussions of country life in "the good old days".

The early evenings were spent gathering sticks and twigs for Molly, so she could start the fire, her big hands building up the fuel as he sat in the corner and turned the handle of the Pierce fan.

Once, when he expressed concern that she might burn herself, she smiled and said,

"Ah sure, I'm fireproof boy."

Then it was delicious home-made currant bread and sweet tea followed by an hour or two ensconced in one of the cosy seats set into the chimney, listening to the large battery-powered radio on the fold-down trestle table, and watching the smoke curl up through the great chimney before he was packed off to the high feather bed he would share with Tom.

Tom would be away at the local pub and would come in late. Pat, barely awake, would peer out at him from the warm feather bed, and watch him empty his pockets of large copper coins and place them in neat piles on a shelf over the door near where an ancient shotgun hung.

Pat's eyes would flicker, become heavy, and he would drift off to sleep again. When he awoke, the cock would have long ceased crowing, and Tom would have gone to milk the cows.

For the rest of the week Pat fed the chickens, helped Molly make butter in the little dairy, carried the buckets from the milking parlour with Tom, and, when Tom was not in sight, surreptitiously climbed the hay stacks.

On another occasion he helped Tom turn the sheaves of corn in the fields, an exciting activity as various small rodents fled from their hiding place and were chased by Tom's mongrel, Spot.

When there were no chores to be done, he borrowed a couple of jam jars from Molly, and spent hours catching small fish from the little stream, ambitiously named the Douglas River, which ran through the farmyard.

The last day of his stay was a Friday, and that night, as a special treat, Tom brought him to the local pub, and sat him in the corner of the bar with a large bottle of lemonade, while he took his usual place in the weekly card-game.

The following morning, by some coincidence, his mother arrived in the car, and he eagerly jumped in beside her, tired and happy, but pleased to be going home…..

After a number of years in the big cities of the world, Ryan returned to Ireland, anxious to exchange his high pressure job in Canada for a laid back life in Ireland. But Ireland had changed too, and paying for a house, a car and children's school fees took up a lot more time and effort than he had expected.

There had been changes in Ballyvoreen too. Poor Tom had died and Molly lived alone in the thatched farmhouse.

Ryan's mother had long passed away, along with most of Molly's contemporaries. She no longer cycled to town but took the bus when she felt up to it.

Ryan visited her now and again, but not as often as he should have. She welcomed him with some of the warm good humour of former years, but then began to speak bitterly of her lost opportunities, her sorrow of never marrying, of never having the security and intimacy of a partner in life, someone to be by her side, to share the good times and the bad. She deeply regretted that she had returned from the United States. Her life stopped going anywhere after that. Now an old woman, life had nothing for her. Here she was, in her eighties, still gathering twigs and sticks for the fire.

Ryan was saddened by her state of mind and, instead of giving his strength when hers was fading, he allowed his own problems to take precedence and saw her less and less.

He heard she had gone into a nursing home, and then, full of good intentions to go and see her, he heard she had died suddenly.

At the funeral he had stood at the back of the church, and went home early…..

Brrrrrrrrrrrrrng!

The bell of the electric cooker jolted Ryan from his thoughts.

He went into the kitchen and turned the cooker off before returning to his armchair and picking up the leather-bound book.

He glanced again at the note written on the scrap of green-lined paper.

"To be passed on to Pat Ryan who is related to the O'Briens"

How wrong the writer was.

SECOND VIOLIN

Murphy sat in the sagging armchair and stared out the front window of number 11 Alma Place. The rain showed no sign of stopping and if anything looked like it would continue into the night. Across the road he saw a woman painstakingly park her car in a tiny space on the narrow street, and then enter the house opposite after juggling in the wet gloom with various locks and keys. In the darkness of her hall he could see the security light flashing as she rushed to turn off the alarm. The heavy door slammed behind her.

Another dreary November evening.

He decided not to go down to the pub and spend another evening listening to the loud voices of the young while hoping one of his pals might drop in. Not that he was old he told himself. Thirty-eight wasn't old. It used to be considered middle-aged but these days fifty-five to sixty-five is considered middle-aged. Well, in some quarters anyway, and according to *Hello* magazine.

Still, it was a fact that most of his friends were married or in "a long-term relationship" he reflected,

126

mentally wagging the first two fingers on each hand. And, as a statistician, he knew that 74% of all men aged thirty-eight or over were married. That was why most of his friends only rarely showed up at the pub. They were at home presumably, building their nests with their partners, getting ready for Christmas.

He walked over to the television and switched it on. Glancing through the TV guide, he noted that most of the programmes were repeats, and he'd seen all the films before. He flicked through the channels, watched *The Simpsons* for twenty minutes, and then listened to David Attenborough whispering from behind a bush as the television showed a lesser-spotted African hyena make crunchingly short work of a young Thompson's gazelle.

After that he was about to turn off the TV when the continuity presenter announced that that there had been a change in the programme and they would now be showing a recording of the concert held in the National Concert Hall a few weeks before, featuring Beethoven's Symphonies Number 5 and 6.

Hm, thought Murphy, the first two pieces of classical music I ever bought, nearly twenty years ago—not that his classical collection had increased to any great extent over the subsequent years. Still, it might be worth watching.

He dashed into the small kitchen, made a quick ham and chutney sandwich, and having put the kettle on, returned to the living room.

The announcer had just finished his preamble and the orchestra had started immediately into the first sombre C minor movement of the 5th Symphony—bohm, bohm, bohm, bohmmmm—"Fate knocking on the door."

Murphy made himself comfortable on the sofa, with the day's newspaper on his lap to catch the crumbs and odd bits of chutney from his sandwich.

The music was beautifully played, the grim wartime association remembered, although the music reflected another, earlier war, and another earlier despot. The sound was excellent, the TV picture perfect.

He began to lose himself in the great power of the music, the exquisite and fine teamwork of the orchestra as the camera moved from one corner of the stage to the other.

Quite often the camera paused at the front row of the string section and he recognized the familiar face of the lady who was the orchestra leader, now a national treasure, revered by the Dublin 4 set. Slightly at an angle behind her sat one of the second violins, an unfamiliar figure, but certainly an attractive one.

The camera switched to a bassoon player, a stout gentleman with a shiny bald head and red cheeks which grew redder in proportion to the demands of his part of the music. The timpani were visited and then back to the violin section.

There was something about that second violin, a small, slim young woman with a shock of black hair which covered her face as she swayed to and fro, vigorously playing her part of the demanding symphony.

She wore a tight-fitting, black velvet dress with long sleeves and a high collar. It wasn't ostentatious, but its silver sheen showed her lithe figure and slim waist to perfection as she moved backwards and forwards with the music. Her breasts were small but proud thought Murphy— who considered himself an expert in these matters— and in perfect proportion to her body, while entirely in keeping with her narrow waist and flat stomach. Her feet were crossed at the ankles and tucked under her seat.

The camera whipped away but was back again in no time. The cameraman could have been making sure that the orchestra leader was getting the maximum cover due to her, but Murphy was convinced that he was ogling the young second violin.

He had almost lost track of the music when the orchestra moved into the fourth movement and the triumphant C major finalé. The cameras now concentrated on the percussion, the trombones and the lone piccolo, with just an occasional glimpse of the violins as the symphony came to an end.

Murphy dashed to the kitchen, re-started the kettle, found a slightly stale piece of chester-bread cake in the bread box, and was back in front of the television as the melodious early strains of the Pastoral Symphony began.

Forty minutes later Murphy was in love.

"Cop yourself on," he told himself. But there was something about that small female figure that attracted and fascinated him.

"Is it because she is so tiny?" he asked himself.

The cliché "but perfectly formed" entered his mind.

Or was it the fact that he could not quite see her face behind that dark, gleaming, auburn hair?

He watched the orchestra take a bow, and then another. But it was most frustrating. Every time the second violin was about to brush the hair from her face the camera switched to the conductor or another part of the orchestra. Then the credits rolled up as the program came to an end.

"Shit and derision" swore Murphy, throwing the remote control on the sofa.

Still, life had to continue, and Murphy went to bed early and was up at the break of day, and off to his job in the Department of Statistics.

His office was in a grey building close to the Department of Finance. The long expected refurbishment of his office had not yet materialised and numerous files lay piled on his wooden desk and on the solid oak shelves which ranged around the room. The computer into which he gazed was the only sign of modernity, and its screen was covered with lists of figures which would be puzzling to the uninitiated, but which Murphy knew were the statistics relating to the number of unmarried couples co-habitating in new houses, and which he was now updating from the recent census.

Although his eyes were on the screen his mind was elsewhere. At the National Concert Hall in fact, where the image of the violinist in velvet had first appeared.

By the end of the week Murphy had done very little work but he had booked a ticket to the regular Friday night concert featuring the National Symphony Orchestra.

On Friday he left the office at five and rushed home, treating himself to a 'fry' for tea—two eggs, four sausages, two rashers and a couple of buttered slices of fresh white bread.

After immersing his skinny body in the shower he had a fresh shave and exchanged his slightly shiny workaday suit for what he regarded as 'arty' clothes— black jeans, a black cord shirt and black leather slip-on shoes. He examined his own transformation in the mirror, frowning slightly as he leaned forward to look at an incipient boil on the side of his nose and resolving to cut back on fries. Still, not a bad looking fellow, he thought, applying some stinging after-shave. He pulled on a black leather jacket and headed of at a brisk pace to the National Concert Hall at Earlsfort Terrace.

When he arrived, he found a cheerful crowd of classical music enthusiasts of all ages and backgrounds milling about in the foyer. The buzz of conversation was punctuated by the tinkle of glasses and a queue had formed at the bar .

Tonight they were to hear music by Edward Elgar, always a popular choice, and all seats were sold out. Murphy had been lucky to obtain a seat at all, but found himself at the back of the stalls, on the left-hand side. To his disgust he realised that he had a very limited view of his violinist, limited still further by the presence, in the seat in front of him, of a large gentleman with a shock of grey hair urgently in need of treatment for dandruff.

At the interval, Murphy returned as quickly as he could to the foyer and made his way up the corridor to what was known as the Band Room. Here a surly looking security man held the door open for the members of the orchestra as they filed into the room, chattering away to each other and surreptitiously lighting up cigarettes, in spite of the presence of numerous NO SMOKING signs. The men were all wearing tuxedos and the women were dressed in black, mostly long, dresses. There was no sign of the second violin. Presumably she would have been amongst the first to leave the stage and had already entered the room. When the door closed finally, Murphy continued to loiter, intently scrutinising his program. The security man had moved a few yards down the corridor, speaking into his noisy handset, and Murphy found that, if he stood at a certain angle he could just see through the crack between the two doors of the Band Room.

But there was no sign of Alice Arcesi, as he had

discovered from the program was the name of the young violinist.

By the time the bell rang urging patrons to return to their seats the security man was bombarding Murphy with dirty looks. A minute or two later the double doors of the Band Room swung open releasing a cloud of smoke and a crowd of noisy musicians—he recognised the red-faced, baldy bassoon player. The surly security man had now placed himself importantly between Murphy and the orchestra members as they streamed past and into the auditorium. Murphy did not even catch a glimpse of his violinist, who, being so small, was completely hidden from view in the phalanx of tuxedos and long, black dresses.

He returned to his seat, and settled down to enjoy the Cello Concerto, always a deeply moving piece of music, but in this new circumstance in which he found himself, enthralled by someone he didn't even know, almost unbearably sad. The guest cellist, a superbly talented young Englishman, thrilled the audience, but Murphy's eyes remained on Alice throughout the concerto. When it came to an end the audience gave a standing ovation, and Murphy blew his nose noisily into a man-size tissue.

As the crowd moved toward the exits, Murphy impatiently squeezed his way through them, anxious to be at the front doors when Alice came through. He almost ran through the great foyer, knocking a glass from one man's hand in the process. Reaching the main door, he placed himself in a position outside on the steps to see all who came out.

It began to rain. Just a few drops at first but gradually increasing. Murphy pulled up the collar of his jacket. Nearly ten minutes passed before he realised that the musicians were leaving from a separate door near the corner of the building. He walked as fast as he could to the corner cursing his own stupidity. Quite a few members of the orchestra were still streaming out. Some stood on the footpath and hailed taxies, others were being picked up by family or friends.

Then he saw Alice, walking by herself in the direction of Leeson Street. The rain was now pouring down and she looked small and vulnerable holding the collar of her light coat up around her neck. He walked faster, wondering if he should catch up with her and talk to her about the concert. But just then she saw a bus about to move off at the corner of Stephen's Green and ran for it, her scarf blowing from her shoulders just as she jumped onto the moving platform. Murphy scooped up the scarf and ran after the bus, but it was moving too fast, the driver anxious to finish his shift.

She looked back, saw him with the scarf and smiled, then shrugged as she realised he could not catch up with the bus. As she stood there, holding on to the railing, her hair blew away from her face revealing a livid birth mark all down one side of it. But she smiled and called out,

"Leave it in the box office if that's O.K. ?"

134

He stopped running and, caught for breath, nodded vehemently.

He barely heard the words "Thank you" as she turned into the bus which roared down Stephen's Green in a cloud of diesel fumes and rain.

Murphy watched until the bus disappeared at Harcourt Street corner, then slowly turned around and began to walk back towards the concert hall.

The birth mark had taken him by surprise. Not that there was anything wrong with that he told himself vehemently. She is still a beautiful woman, and brave at that, he thought. Still, he felt a surge of sympathy for her, alone on a bus late on a Friday night, exposed to the jibes and insults of young thugs.

What a pity he did not catch the bus. She probably lives in a flat somewhere on the south side of the city.

He glanced at the fine, white mohair scarf in his hands, instinctively holding it up to his nose. There was a soft scent of perfume from it. He held it against his cheek for a moment, before folding it and returning to the concert hall.

The box office was closed but seeing an elderly lady inside he tapped on the glass and she opened the window. He explained that he had been having a drink with Alice Arcesi after the concert and she had left her scarf behind. He knew that she was fond of it and was anxious to post it to her immediately.

The old lady smiled, sensing romance and thinking how most young men these days wouldn't bother their barney.   Still…

"Have you any identification?" she asked Murphy, peering over her gold spectacles which were held in place by a piece of black material that used to be called knicker elastic.

Murphy took out his civil service parking card— Department of Finance— which the old lady found to be quite impressive.

"Hm…very well, I suppose it would be all right; now here is the address; 2 Maple Crescent, Dundrum. All right now, dear ?"

Murphy thanked the old lady, made a note of the address, and began his walk home. The rain had eased off, the street was washed clean, and there was a fresh smell in the air.

He was surprised to hear she lived on the North side, but lots of students lived there, often in 'digs', as he had himself when he first came to Dublin.

He spent a restless night in bed, unable to settle down and sleep, constantly trying to decide what he should do next. Early in the morning he finally surrendered and fell into a very deep trance, half awakened from time to time by his own rattling snores.

It was near midday before the sun streaming into his bedroom window woke him up. After a long shower and a breakfast of stale bread and marmalade, he decided that the only thing to do was to go to Dundrum, return the scarf, and take Alice out to dinner.

This time he opted for the casual look, pulling on a pair of blue jeans and a lumberjack shirt. He took the bus to Dundrum, and got off at the post office there, where he enquired as to the whereabouts of Maple Crescent. The postmistress gave him detailed directions—apparently it was a good 15 minute walk—telling him that when he got to the end of Dolmen Road, he should turn right and he would be in Maple Crescent.

Murphy set off. The route took him through streets of modest Victorian and Edwardian houses, most of them very well maintained. He arrived at Dolmen Road and continued walking, noting that there were fewer houses here, but a number of run-down timber sheds with tarred roofs. Most of them seemed to be empty, with gaping holes in their sides. A number of abandoned cars were scattered here and there, stripped of anything of use.

Murphy was surprised, and wondered what kind of a place was Alice living in ?

At last he came to the end of Dolmen Road. His curiosity mounting, he turned right, past a concrete building with a faded sign indicating that a mechanic was always on duty. Two smashed and rusty petrol pumps stood outside the boarded up windows. Just beyond that was a huge, brightly coloured sign on two poles which said,

WELCOME TO MAPLE CRESCENT –
Superb 4–bedroom detached houses.

Two freshly planted, pencil-thin maples flanked the sign. Beyond it, a crescent of thirty or forty dazzling new bungalows stretched out of sight.

Murphy only paused for a moment. Well, number two can't be far away he thought, walking past the first bungalow which appeared to be unoccupied.

A shiny new car was parked outside the second. He walked up to the front door. Two unconnected wires were where the bell should have been. There was no knocker. He flicked the flap of the letter box a few times but no one answered. He could hear music playing in the house, but no one came to the door when he rapped on it with his knuckles.

He cautiously walked around to the back of the building, to what appeared to be the kitchen window, and peeped in.

The music was much louder now, a symphony orchestra playing Mozart. Alice stood in the middle of the kitchen at an ironing board, seemingly singing along with the music. Her hair was tied back, and Murphy thought that she was even more pretty with her birthmark. She was wearing faded jeans and a white blouse, and was making short work of a pile of laundry.

Murphy smiled.

Just then, a door from the dining room to the kitchen flew open and in tottered a small child with curly black hair bawling, "Mammy, Mammy"

He or she seemed to have spilled the entire contents of an infant's painting set over his or her self.

Alice turned to the child, cooing in sympathy and using one of the freshly washed hand-towels to clean its face.

Murphy was taken aback.

The door swung open again and in ran a mischievous looking pair of twin girls a few years older than the first child.

"We didn't do it Mammy, honestly Mammy" they squealed.

Murphy, now beginning to feel a complete fool, thought they looked the image of Alice.

As he crouched, looking in wonder at the little domestic scene, the dining room door swung open once more and in walked a tall red-faced man who looked strangely familiar.

"Christ!" thought Murphy to himself, "It's the baldy bassoon player!"

The bassoon player began to tickle the children and then Alice. They all roared with laughter.

Stunned, Murphy turned away and walked down the short driveway to the road.

"What a bloody fool I am!" he thought.

He was in such a daze that he did not see the builder's van coming towards him. It struck him a glancing blow and spun him into the gutter. Murphy felt an agonising pain in his right leg and fainted.

When he recovered, just a minute or two later, there was a small crowd around him. The van driver had put his cement-dusty coat under Murphy's head and Alice was holding his hand, dabbing a nasty graze with a freshly laundered towel.

"Don't worry, my husband has called the ambulance" she said, smiling down at him. She obviously didn't recognise him, and under the circumstances, it simply did not occur to Murphy to take the scarf out of his pocket and give it to her.

The ambulance was very quick. With the help of Alice and her husband, the driver and the nurse loaded Murphy onto a stretcher and took him into the vehicle. Having checked his injuries they gave him a mild painkiller and drove off towards the hospital.

The painkiller made Murphy feel a bit groggy and somehow even more stupid. His head lolled, and the nurse leaned over to straighten the pillow.

She had a slim and attractive figure, Murphy noted, trying to look up, and focusing his eyes he observed her well manicured hands and tanned skin as she checked his pulse.

He couldn't quite see her face. As she leaned over in the moving ambulance it was completely covered by her beautiful, long, blonde hair….

THE CRUISE OF THE CONDOR

The early morning sun lit up Roaring Water Bay, the islands, and the approaches to the pier at Schull.

A stiff South-Easterly wind moved the few clouds in scudding tufts over Mount Gabriel.

A large motor-sailer was moored at the pier, its brilliant white hull sharply reflected in the blue-green choppy waters, its halliards rattling and ringing against the mainmast.

Kennedy looked around the deck. Everything seemed in order. All the ropes on deck were beautifully coiled, the fenders were in their proper places, and all gear surplus to requirements was stored down below.

Now, where the hell is McFadden? He peered up the narrow street leading to the pier. Still no sign of his crewman.

He took out a red handkerchief with white polka dots and briskly polished his spectacles before glancing up at the mainmast.

Ah yes, he thought, we must hoist the burgee.

He went to a locker and took from it, neatly folded,

the red burgee of the Royal Cork Yacht Club, the oldest yacht club in the world. There are one or two more we could hoist also, he mused, but the Royal Cork will do fine.

He went below and for the sixth time checked that all the stores and supplies were in order. In the neat, mahogany-panelled galley, a row of wine glasses gleamed at him from their individual cubbyholes.

He returned to the deck and thought again about McFadden, and reflected on the occasional trips he had made with McFadden as crew. He stepped onto the pier and sat on a bollard and reflected on "The Cruise of the *Condor*," as he liked to call the trip of a few years ago (in a much smaller boat) which was to have been a pleasant cruise but soon turned into an ordeal……..

Kennedy had inherited the *Condor*, a well-maintained but ancient, clinker-built folkboat, from his late father.

In his father's time the boat had been immaculately maintained, and, in spite of its small size and primitive accommodation, run like a royal yacht.

On certain specific days in the month of August, Regatta Day and the like, Commodore Kennedy and his 'man', both well past seventy-five, and both rather formally dressed (the Commodore in his blazer and white ducks, and his man, taking the lead from his boss, in Sunday suit and black shoes) rowed out to where the *Condor* was moored and, with a certain amount of gasping, clambered aboard.

Quite some time would pass while the two old men, working with the quiet confidence of experience, pressed their arthritic fingers into hauling out sails and battens, sheets and halyards, and fixing them in place.

Eventually, the jib and mainsail would be slowly hauled to the top of the mast, where with a crack and billow they would take the wind, and, mooring dropped, the *Condor* would sail serenely out of the harbour, her two satisfied seadogs puffing gently in the cockpit.

In the fullness of time, both men crossed the great bar in the sky and the *Condor* was hauled out of the water and stored in a warehouse.

Kennedy was determined however, that his father's old boat should return to the sea, and approached a reputable boatyard to see what could be done to restore the *Condor* to her original condition. The shipwright went over the boat with the nautical equivalent of a fine tooth comb and, over a period of two years, Kennedy was relieved of considerable sums of money as the boat underwent a refit. Her knees were examined, along with her bottom, and all that should be replaced was, until finally it was time for phase two of his plan, which was to sail the boat to what would be her summer station in West Cork.

The *Condor*, woodwork gleaming and brass shining, was duly lowered into the water at Dunmore East and the moment her hull had settled great spouts of water began to appear inside the boat. She had been out of the water for so long that her planks had dried and shrunk and she was full of leaks. This contingency had been planned for however and a Honda pump was placed on board to pump the water out. This soon had to be joined by another pump before the rate of outflow matched the rate of inflow. The whole operation was placed in the hands of a local man who was an expert in these things.

In twenty-four hours only one pump was required as the wood began to swell, and in another thirty-six hours the one pump was needed only occasionally

Meanwhile a crew had to be organised, but for some reason this proved to be difficult. One or two friends came to help him get the boat rigged. He noticed them glancing at the soaking interior and the rather cramped conditions before they rolled out their excuses. One had promised his wife that he would clean up the garden. Another remembered a book launch he had promised to attend.

Kennedy was delighted therefore when, having rung McFadden and offered him a cruise down to Schull, County Cork, he was answered with an enthusiastic yes.

On the appointed Friday afternoon, McFadden arrived with an assortment of bags, sailing clothes, bright yellow sailing boots and a life jacket. When most of these had been struck down below—with some difficulty as storage space was limited—Kennedy brought him around the boat and introduced him to his duties.

Although by no means an expert, McFadden had sailed before and knew the basics. He just needed reminding from time to time, and speed was unknown to him. With his beard and an American naval officer's cap he had acquired somewhere, he at least looked the part.

On the day of departure all went well and by mid-morning the *Condor* was sailing westwards in a gentle Easterly breeze. They were obviously not going to break any records on this cruise, and Sebastian accepted the fact that they would have to heave-to at Ballycotton and spend the night there.

Meanwhile, they caught up on each other's news, pumped out the bilges every half hour, and examined the cliffs and rocks that passed slowly by on their starboard side like a never-ending theatrical stage setting.

Here and there on the sharp rocks on the shore a cormorant stood, holding out its wings to dry as it gazed with reptilian eyes at the passing yacht.

From time to time Kennedy squinted up at the burgee, polishing his spectacles with his handkerchief and watching for a change in the wind.

At 4 0'clock, McFadden took the helm and watched while Kennedy very precisely set the little table in the cockpit with cold meat, cheese and lettuce before reaching down into the bilges and taking up a bottle of white wine. (Cecil noted how fastidiously Kennedy dusted their two mugs with his handkerchief, and later unobtrusively rinsed his mug over the side when Kennedy was preoccupied with the wine bottle).

They both enjoyed the food and wine and had just tidied up when Ballycotton Island came into view. This was a large, rocky pile on which a lighthouse and coastguard station stood. A couple of hundred yards away, across the water, was the tiny port of Ballycotton, home of a few small fishing vessels, two pubs and a hotel.

Kennedy pondered for a minute or two and then made a decision. They would anchor outside the pier, and then take the little dingy, which had been towed behind the *Condor,* and row into the small sheltered harbour.

All went well, and two hours later the two of them were ensconced in the little chintzy hotel beside the pier, perusing the somewhat limited but generous menu.

The atmosphere was warm and comfortable, and Kennedy enjoyed a Pims No. I while McFadden lowered a pint of Guinness, before both tucked into steak, potatoes and mixed vegetables which seemed to be the specialty of the house.

Afterwards in the bar, the two men enjoyed a night-cap.

The smoky room was full of locals and a bit of a sing-song began. *The Fields of Athenry* was followed by *Four Green Fields*, and then a very old fisherman with a cap shiny with age sang a sad ballad in Irish which had everyone wiping a tear from their eye. The two yachtsmen didn't understand the song but, taking their cue from the locals, looked grave and nodded their heads approvingly.

In spite of Kennedy's best efforts to restrain him, McFadden then sang his favourite (and only) song, *The Summer Time is Coming*. This went down quite well, the locals clapping politely, and McFadden, with a gleam in his eye, was about to order another round, while trying to remember the words of another song, when Kennedy grabbed him and hauled him out into the night.

The two men untied the dingy from the pier and rowed across to the *Condor*. The wind had died down, to be replaced by a heavy dew. The cabin was decidedly damp and cold after the snug hotel, but they climbed into the sleeping bags in their bunks with a certain satisfaction, warmed by food and alcohol, and were rocked asleep by the faint movement of the hull on the almost dead calm waters.

Kennedy was awakened the next morning by the movement of McFadden about the cabin muttering "beat to quarters – beat to quarters" (he was a great fan of the works of Patrick O'Brian). But in fairness, he already had a frying pan going on the little gas stove and a wonderful aroma of fried bacon lingered on the morning air.

The wind had picked up, so they finished their breakfast as quickly as possible, picked up their anchor, manoeuvred out from Ballycotton Island, and continued their voyage.

The wind had indeed freshened, but had veered so that it was no longer behind them but was striking them at an angle on the port bow. The sea had changed too, and deep troughs and large white horses were the order of the day. They carried on, the mast at a sharp angle, the mainsail boom hauled in tight to make the most of an unfriendly wind.

Normally the boat would have no trouble with these winds but another problem revealed itself dramatically.

As the *Condor* heeled over to the stronger winds, water began to pour in through the upper timbers of the hull, revealing a serious oversight in Kennedy's otherwise meticulous preparations for the voyage.

The upper planks of the hull had never had a chance to soak and swell as the boat sat in the calm waters of Dunmore East Harbour. Now, every time the boat heeled, rivulets of water poured freely into the cockpit and cabin.

McFadden immediately began pumping as Kennedy juggled the helm and sails in an attempt to keep the boat as upright as possible. It was hard work for both of them, but neither suggested heading for the shore.

The entrance to Cork Harbour appeared and was passed, and by the time the Bulman Rock, which guarded the entrance to the Kinsale river, came into view, the wind was close to gale force and rain was falling.

Kennedy, handing McFadden a large brass crankhandle, asked him to go forward on the coach roof and reef the mainsail. This was a relatively simple matter, in calm waters, of inserting the crankhandle in the mast and winding it so that the boom would turn and roll up the sail on itself. However, the coach roof was wet and slippery, and the boat was heaving up and down.

Along with the brass crankhandle, Kennedy offered McFadden an ancient canvas webbing belt (rather like something a soldier might wear on the Western Front, thought McFadden) and promised a bottle of champagne on arrival in Kinsale, but McFadden shrugged the verdigris coated belt aside, although he was feeling far from brave, and grasping the crankhandle, went forward to the mast on hands and knees, where, drenched by the spray from the plunging bow, he managed to reef in a considerable part of the mainsail.

The action of the boat settled immediately, and she became more manageable. But Kennedy had spotted another problem.

Half a mile out from the entrance to the Kinsale River, a motor cruiser lay, bobbing up and down in the troughs, obviously not under power.

Kennedy declared that they had no option but to go and see if assistance was required.

The exhausted McFadden, still working the pump, groaned but conceded that Kennedy might be right.

Between frantic bouts at the bilge pump he gathered up air-filled cushions which doubled as life preservers and listened to Kennedy's instructions.

Kennedy would take the *Condor* around the stern of the powerless motor cruiser, and put McFadden in a position to throw the life preservers to the occupants.

Then Kennedy, with considerable difficulty, changed course twice before positioning the *Condor* to pass by the stern of the motor cruiser. At last the moment came when they pounded through the short, sharp swells and drew abreast of the cruiser's stern. They both glanced at the cruiser, expecting perhaps to see a distraught couple with two young children cowering in the wheelhouse. Instead they saw two elderly gentlemen, well clothed in oilskins, sitting in the cockpit, their fishing rods extended over the stern. One of them, a pipe in the corner of his mouth, smiled and waved a friendly greeting before adjusting the slack of his line. The other just smiled.

Kennedy turned and glared at McFadden before pushing the tiller over. The *Condor* heeled and surged forward towards the entrance to Kinsale harbour.

McFadden waved farewell to the two old gents in the motor cruiser.

"McFadden, get up for'ard and prepare to drop the jib" roared Kennedy.

McFadden had just lowered the jib when Kennedy roared again;

"Get aft man and get that pump going or we'll be bloody well swamped."

McFadden heaved and puffed over the bilge pump.

Once into the river the sails were useless and more drama ensued as Kennedy, with great difficulty, got the one-cylinder petrol engine going.

Now blinded by a combination of petrol fumes and spray, he feverishly cleaned his glasses with his polka dotted handkerchief.

"McFadden, get for'ard and tell me where we're going."

McFadden again ran forward to the bow and shouted instructions to his skipper through a cloud of blue smoke.

More by luck than good management they found an empty berth at the marina, and slowly glided in, the little engine misfiring continually and noisily, and producing a cloud of toxic smoke which clung around them, the wind having been reduced by rising headlands on each side of the bay.

They tied up fore and aft and immediately set about dismantling the mainsail and stowing it away.

In the middle of their labours a pretty girl leaned over the side of a large motor cruiser moored beside them (which Kennedy had referred to disdainfully as a 'floating gin palace') and invited them aboard for cocktails. The clink of glasses and the buzz of conversation could be heard coming from a roomy

151

cabin.

"No, no, thank you, we have work to do" said Kennedy.

McFadden sighed and smiled at the girl, shrugging his shoulders like a Frenchman. He would have considered committing murder in exchange for a large glass of gin and tonic.

Later, as Kennedy kept repeating the term "everything must be ship-shape and Bristol Fashion", every single bit of rope, sail, pot or pan had been tied with a cord and stored in precisely the place designated for it.

The two men then put on dry clothes and prepared to go ashore.

Kennedy looked at his sodden wallet, frowned and said to McFadden,

"Look here Mac, about that bottle of champagne, will you settle for a pint of stout?"

"Well, if I must " said McFadden, who at this stage would have cheerfully consumed a pint of anti-freeze, cold or not.

He smiled to himself, jumped out onto the pontoon and headed for the sailing club bar.

Kennedy frowned, then jumped onto the pontoon and followed him, shouting,

"Hang on McFadden, it's my round you know!"

A SEA CHANGE

The sea spread out before him in the moonlight, black with a scattering of silver dust, the wave crests an almost florescent white in the light of the full moon. Black valleys interspersed with silver mountain ridges, constantly moving, surging, sliding away into the distance.

Michael sat half slumped in the captains seat, his legs wrapped around its supports, the slow, heavy roll of the ship urging him to sleep, to abandon this monotonous watch and give himself to the eternity which would almost certainly follow if he did.

He rubbed his eyes and forced himself to stare through the frost-cleaned windscreen, the bow rising slowly, rolling ponderously on a frothy crest, only to tip over, and, with gathering speed, slide deep into the black trough for the millionth time.

And yet, he looked forward to this time, in the grave-yard watch, almost alone on the bridge, the ship under his control, the high winds and seas protecting him from attack from below, and the night, though brightened by the moon, casting a thin, black, protective cloak over his movements.

As his eyes, heavy with fatigue, almost robot-like, scanned the horizon, his mind would reflect on the monotonous predictability of his life, the sheer drudgery and routine which made up the bulk of it, the moments of fear and lack of confidence in himself which made up the rest.

He clutched his mug of tea, enjoying the small gift of heat which seeped into his hands.

From the port side a renegade wave creamed over the forward turret, causing the ship to stagger like a drunken man who has just struck a lamp-post, before resuming its forward motion.

He dropped the mug and grasped the wooden armrests with both hands. Away on the starboard beam, beyond the moonlit wave crests and in the murk of the horizon, a tiny flash passed unnoticed.

The next two flashes registered on his retina. There were no more, even though he searched the area for over five minutes with his night glasses.

There was something about the flashes which tugged at his brain, a touch of colour in an otherwise black and white landscape. He unhooked the blower to the captain's cabin.

"Two flashes sir, away to starboard…….no, just two, I'm fairly certain…"

The captain sounded very tired on the blower. He

muttered some instructions. Michael listened, nodding, his eyes closed.

"Very well sir, we'll keep a sharp look-out."

Michael put the whistle back in the blower and hung it on the bulkhead. After a while he felt his eyes losing all comprehension of what they were seeing. Black became white, and white black. His mind wandered, contrasting this night with others, some real, some dreamt, some a mixture of reality and some founded on reports he had read; ships lost with all hands, convoys abandoned, tankers blown sky-high. Dozens of pitiful, mauled survivors being hauled out of the sea to suffer a few hours of agony, their pains hardly assuaged by the meager supply of drugs available.

He recalled that awful night when the ship had engine trouble and lay silent, alone on the sea, powerless, a wingless fly on a liquid web; a paralysed water beetle on a huge lake full of young pike.

There had been a full moon that night too, although the sea remained as calm as a garden pond. The crew had left their bunks and huddled on the deck wrapped in blankets. Some had small bags containing whatever was precious to them. In dark corners near one of the gun turrets and in the shelter of the bridge forbidden cigarettes glowed.

Deep in the ship the repairs proceeded apace, the engineer's muffled hammer tolling like a distant funeral bell. A spare section of the shaft, gleaming under its coat of oil and grease, was manhandled below, silently, carefully and lovingly.

An hour before dawn the engineer reported that repairs had been completed. The captain thanked him and rang for Full Speed Ahead…...

Michael stopped his head from hitting his chest. He took his eyes from the streaming seas and looked at his watch. Nearly time to turn in, to fall into that damp bed and drag the crumpled blankets over himself. To sleep, 'perchance to dream,' for a few hours at least.

Faces drifted through his mind's eye. Comrades, some became friends, many he barely knew. Some moved away and were never seen again. Others lived in close proximity to him but he never saw them.

He closed his eyes and yawned—time to turn in. Almost nodding off he reached for the button to summon his replacement.

More flashes! Orange flashes! This time really close! He shook his head.

His mother walked into the room and took the clicker from his hand.

"Mikie, will you for God's sake leave that old video alone and go and give your dad a hand! He wants to take the car in off the road and put it in the garage. It's pouring rain and he's been flashing his lights for the past ten minutes. What have you been looking at, another war story is it? Well, I'll give you another war story if you don't get up off that sofa and get down the yard!"

****